B.A.E. 2

Before Anyone Else

By

Jahquel J.

Published by Royalty Publishing House
www.royaltypublishinghouse.com

Contains explicit language & adult themes suitable for ages 16+

Be sure to LIKE our Royalty Publishing House page on Facebook

Chapter One

Moet

I sat in the middle of Zane's bed watching TV, while stealing glances at my engagement ring. I still couldn't believe I was going to be a married woman soon, but I couldn't help but feel like I shouldn't be happy. My best friend, Tammy was going through one of the worst things in her life, and here I was at my happiest I've ever been. I turned the TV off and lay down on the pillow, while looking out the floor-to-ceiling windows of the city. I couldn't sleep without Zane in the bed with me, but he had to fly out to California to handle a couple things. I wanted to call him, but I didn't want to keep calling and nagging him. I sat up on the bed and grabbed my phone. Just as I was about to slide my finger across the screen, Ki's number popped up. I rolled my eyes and answered.

"What?" I said, not bothering to hide my annoyance.

"Damn, it's like that now, Moe?" he said, and I looked at the phone.

"Nigga, it's been like that. It's been like that since you fucked Blake's nasty ass. Get the fuck off my line, because I'm sure my man wouldn't like it!" I yelled, and ended the call.

In a quick minute, he managed to fuck up my night. I slammed my phone on the nightstand and laid down and looked up at the ceiling. My phone started buzzing, so I grabbed it and answered, without looking at the screen.

"What the fuck you want?" I yelled, not caring at all.

"Moet?" my supervisor's voice came through the phone.

"My bad, Clarence. What's up?" I said, calming down. I prayed he didn't want me to come in tonight, because I didn't feel like it.

"Your sister came in earlier. She was in a car accident-"

"What the fuck you mean earlier? Why am I just now being called?" I hollered, jumping out the bed and putting on a pair of leggings and boots. I was looking a mess and I didn't care. I had on a pair of leggings, Timbs with dress socks, and a crop top.

"I just came on shift, and the other supervisor didn't know she was related to you. I remembered her from the hospital's Christmas party. They called her emergency contact already, but since I didn't see you up here, I figured you didn't know."

"Her emergency contact? Who the hell is that if it isn't me or my parents?"

"Her boyfriend, Jonathan, and his mother," he read to me, and I almost lost my mind.

"I'm on my way now, Clarence. Thanks for calling me," I said, and grabbed my keys and headed out the door.

Soon as I opened the door, I bumped right into Zane's security guard. He looked down at me, as I tried to get around his big ass. "Move it," I snapped, but he didn't move.

"Where are you going, Ms. Rubbins?"

"My sister was in an accident; I need to get to the hospital ASAP!" I screamed, and he held his big ass hand in my face. He said something into his walkie talkie and grabbed my hand.

We made our way downstairs and paparazzi was outside. It was ten at night, and they were still outside the damn building. I rushed past the paparazzi, and one put a microphone in my face.

"Go the fuck home, damn bums!" I yelled and closed the door. I didn't know if I could ever be used to them, but I was willing to put up with them for Zane's sake. I grabbed my phone and dialed my house phone. My father answered sounding half asleep.

"Moet, what the hell you want?" he asked, laughing.

"Daddy, Monett was in a car accident, I'm on my way there now," I explained, and I could hear my mother asking him what was going on.

"What? When? I'm on my way right now. What hospital?"

"My hospital," I said, feeling like I was going to cry. I was so strong, but when I spoke to my daddy, I felt like a little girl that just needed a hug.

"Me and your mother will be there soon. Your mama kept saying her eye was jumping and she had a bad feeling. Be strong baby, and find out everything before we get there."

"Okay, Daddy," I said and ended the call.

When I looked up, we were pulling up to the hospital. I hopped out and rushed inside. Clarence was already waiting and took me straight to her room, so I didn't have to curse out any staff from being impatient. When we entered her room, my sister was sleeping. She had a slash on the side of cheek, but other than that she looked good.

"How is my nephew and sister?" I whispered, turning to Clarence. He motioned for me to come into the hallway.

"She's fine and thankfully, the baby is alright too. We're just monitoring her and the baby. That airbag saved her life, and whatever shielding she did to her stomach. On her hands she has some bruises, which I'm guessing is because she was shielding her stomach. The car didn't go deep into the ditch, but it went far enough off road where she hit bumps, so we did a CT scan to see if there were any head trauma, and it was clear. She's sleeping because we gave her some pain meds to help with the pain. Tomorrow, she'll feel like a truck ran over her, but she and the baby are fine," he explained, and I sighed a huge relief.

"Thank you so much, Clarence," I thanked him, and hugged him.

"You're welcome. Take some time off and be with your sister. You can go in," he said, and patted me on the shoulder, and walked down the hall to put her charts back up.

I walked back into her room and sat in the chair next to her bed. I gently placed my hands on her bandaged hands. I kissed her on the cheek and sat back down. I was shaking and wondering what happened, and how she got into a ditch. I looked up, and Johnathan and his mother entered the room with food from the cafeteria.

"Oh, we didn't know anyone was here," his mother said, and I looked at her like she had four heads. Johnathan wouldn't even look me in the eyes.

"You didn't know anyone was here? Why wasn't her family called? Johnathan, you blow my house phone up daily, and you couldn't find that number to call me or my parents?"

"Sweetie, if your sister wanted you to know, you would be her emergency contact," his mother spoke up.

I looked at her, and the tray of food she had in her hand. "Baby doll, if you don't mind your business and put the damn tray of food down, because clearly nobody didn't tell you that you look like a stuffed Mrs. Clause. Go find Santa and mind your damn business," I spat, and stood up and crossed my arms.

"Moet, don't disrespect-"

"Nigga, if you don't get out my fuckin' face with disrespect. Your family and yourself disrespected my sister when you were putting hands on her. Did fat ass Mary Poppins step in and help?" I kept my arms folded and paced the room. "Nah, you ignored her pleas for help. Get the fuck out of here with disrespect. You wanna know how I feel about that?" I didn't wait for him to answer, as I decked him right in the face with a right hook. Blood spurted from his face and he held his nose.

"You stupid ass bitch!" He lunged at me, as my father was walking into the room.

"I never liked your ass, so hit my baby girl and I'll lay you out," he said in a low voice, and Johnathan backed away from me. "Get the fuck out and take your mother with you. You have no grounds to be here," he said, and Johnathan took him, his leaking nose and his mother along with him.

"Ugh, I can't stand him, and I'm fading his shit every time I see him," I said, as my father looked at my fist.

"Just like Daddy taught you," he smiled, and then looked at Monett. "How is she?"

After I explained everything to my father, we sat and held her hands. My father made my mother stay home because she was too emotional. He called her sisters over to sit with her, so I felt better knowing she was surrounded by family. I looked down at my phone and forgot I didn't call Hakeem. He deserved to know what happened, since he and Monett were together. I dialed his number and stepped into the hallway.

"What's good, Moe?" he answered, sounding wide awake. I smiled when I heard Zane's voice, but I frowned when I heard music playing. "Are y'all at a party?"

"Yeah, it was a little house warming one of our friends is having. But, what's good?"

"Monett was in an accident. She and the baby is alright, but she isn't awake yet. I just felt you should know," I told him.

"What? When this happen? I'm catching the next flight out, I'll be there by morning," he informed me.

"Okay, I'll send the hospital information."

"Bet." I ended the call and walked back into the room to be with Monett and my father. We sat and held her hands all night. I wanted to know what went down, and I planned to ask as soon as she woke up. I had a feeling that Johnathan had something to do with it.

Cabrina

Thought y'all wouldn't hear from me? Well, you are! Rocky was a mutual friend of Zane and me, so I wasn't surprised when I got an invitation to his house warming/birthday party. I invited my friend, Kareema along with me. She was the baby mama of the big producer, Donovan. We walked into the house and was given a flute of champagne. I was looking super cute in a latex nude dress, with a pair of blush pink heels. My nude Chanel bag matched my outfit. I spotted Rocky over near the bar and walked over to him.

"Look at all that ass in that dress," he said, and spun me around. I had just gotten some more fat taken from my stomach and added to my ass. My shit looked natural, and not like those other bitches.

"You know how I do. Happy birthday, love," I said, handing him a Louis Vuitton gift bag.

"Look at you hooking a nigga up. I appreciate it, ma. Look, I gotta make my rounds, so there's food over there and drinks over there." He pointed to the sections where the refreshments were. "Oh, and your boy here tonight, so don't start nothing. I know your ass," he warned and hugged me.

Kareema walked in front of me and fixed her bra. She had just gotten a breast job, and they looked cute. "He's fine as hell, and I might need his number."

"Ain't you engaged? Stop being a hoe," I laughed, and we walked over to the drinks. I spotted Zane sitting with Hakeem. He looked to be intoxicated, while Hakeem was on the phone with a concerned look on his face.

"Girl, me and my baby been going through shit… What are you looking at?"

I pointed my finger at Hakeem, grabbing his coat and leaving. "That," I smirked, and grabbed two glasses of champagne from the bar.

"Cabrina, leave that nigga alone. He's engaged, and he's just trying to have a good time."

I looked at her like her eyes just fell out her head. "Umm, Kareema, are you his bitch's friend or mine? Because that bitch didn't give a damn about me when she slid up into his life. And engagement? I don't give a fuck about them or their union," I snapped, and left her dumb ass at the bar.

Bitch was over here asking for another nigga's number, but wanted to have some morals when I wanted to go over and talk to Zane. I had to get better with hanging with bitches. My usual home girls had to stay in because of their children so I called her, and now I was realizing it was a mistake. She swore she was the shit since she was on that show, but she had no clue that I had set up a meeting to be on that show as well.

"Hey Zane, I thought you might want a drink," I softly said, and sat beside him. For the first time in months, he didn't screw his face up or insult me with names.

His eyes were low and he was bobbing his head to the music. You could see the stress lines across his face. Maybe it was trouble in paradise. "Preciate it," he said, snatching both cups and guzzling them down.

Since he didn't dismiss me, I crossed my legs and got comfortable. "So how's everything? I haven't spoken to you in a while and that sucks since we were friends before anything else."

He popped open the both of D'Usse sitting in front of us, and poured two cups and handed one to me. He was so drunk that it got on my dress, but it slid off since it was latex. "Stop pressing my girl and we could have remained friends. Why you so hell bent on fucking with us? You still want the dick?" he slurred, grabbing his dick through his pants.

I played with a loose strand of hair and smirked. "I might, but your girl is very violent and ghetto, Zane."

"Nah, she protects what's hers, ain't nothing ratchet and ghetto about that. Plus, her 'ghetto' ass got a college degree," he did air quotes.

I rolled my eyes and took a sip of the drink he offered. I didn't come over here to hear about what his bitch had and did. In my opinion, she wasn't shit because she would be right here with him.

"Whatever, what are you doing tonight?" I asked, as he slugged his drink, and then tilted the bottle and guzzled half the bottle.

"Not you," he laughed, and I rolled my eyes again.

"What happened between us, Zane? I thought we were good, and then I got blindsided by your new chick." I desperately wanted to know. Last I thought we were good, and then he showboats this chick around like I wasn't with him the week before.

"You," he simply replied.

"Me?"

"You too into yourself. I ain't never saw you without makeup or in some basic shit. I need a bitch who gonna be real with me. If you can't be real with yourself, you damn sure can't be real with me."

Even when this nigga was drunk, he still found time to play me. I saw Rocky heading upstairs with another chick, and the party was dying down. I wasn't anywhere near drunk, but apparently Zane was. Since Hakeem left, I decided to take him to his condo that he had in Hollywood; I never went to his house in Beverly Hills.

"Zane, I know I'm the last person you want to be with, but you need someone to take you home," I said, and he nodded his head while still drinking from the bottle. "I'll take you to your condo, and you can come tomorrow and pick up your car." I came up with a solution, as I stood up and pulled my dress down.

He said a couple words that were inaudible, and stood up. It took him a minute to catch his balance, but we walked out the house and got into my car. Kareema had sent me a text and said she was heading home. Thankfully that bitch wasn't with us, because she would have had a lot of smart remarks. I helped him into the car, as he vented about shit I didn't know what he was talking about. I shook my head, and went over to the driver's side and prepared to take the drive from Green Valley to Hollywood.

*

It took a lot of help from his security to help him into the house and into his bedroom. I told them I had it, and helped him out his clothes and got him in the bed. I walked out the room and poured myself a drink, when the bell rang. I went to answer, and it was security. Calvin was Zane's security, and they were tight. He went wherever Zane went.

"Cabrina, I don't know if Zane would want you here when he gets up. I don't think Ms. Moet will either," he brought to my attention, and I guzzled my drink.

"Cal?"

"Yeah," he answered.

"Shut the fuck up. I've been here before his new bitch, and I practically was living here, so you need to really mind your business. Let's wait until he wakes up and asks where the hell you were at, 'cause I was the one who brought him home," I pointed my hand into his big ass chest.

"I-"

"Yeah, save that shit for somebody that cares. Don't disturb us for nothing," I yelled, and slammed the door in his face.

I kicked my heels off, peeled off my dress, and walked around in my thong and bra. Damn, it brought up so many memories walking around. He changed nothing in the condo. I wondered if he brought that bitch here. I bypassed the thought and took my glass of wine back into the bedroom, and got into the bed with him. I scrolled my timeline and looked at Moet's Instagram page. People were worshipping her, and calling me all types of names. Don't get me wrong, I had some die-hard fans that were going hard and flooding her comments with the diamond emoji.

I was fighting the urge to be petty, but overall, the pettiness won. I laid Zane's head on my chest and took a few selfies of us. I kissed his cheek with my red lipstick and took some pictures. Yeah, it was petty and uncalled for, but hey, that bitch deserved that shit. I uploaded the picture and then shut my phone off and his phone off. I didn't want any interruptions. I remember when we used to go to parties together. We would sleep the entire day away with no interruptions. Even if it was for a day, I just needed to be with Zane for once. I snuggled close to him.

"Mmmm, come closer, Moe," he mumbled, and pulled me into him. Although he was calling me another woman, it felt good being in his arms. I closed my eyes and went to sleep. I knew both our phones would be blowing up in the morning.

Moet

Monett finally woke up and I was so happy that I damn near climbed on top of her. She was back to talking shit and acting like herself. Hakeem had made it, and she was so happy to see him. He kept kissing her and questioning her, but she wouldn't tell us what happened. I knew she would in due time, so I wasn't going to stress her about it. As long as both she and my nephew were straight, I didn't care. I tried calling Zane a couple times, but he didn't answer. Tammy had come up and saw Monett, but left because she didn't like to leave Rick's side for too long. I kept looking at my engagement ring and smiling. This is all I ever wanted was to be a man's wife and his everything, and I was finally getting it.

Since the news broke, I had been getting so many phone calls and messages. I had heard from family that I hadn't heard from in years. My phone was going off the charts that my phone was on silent since entering the hospital. I just needed to be with my family and make sure my sister was cool. Clarence said they would be keeping her for another night, and then she would be discharged. I thanked GOD for keeping my sister in his grips, because the outcome could have come out differently. Monett finally made me leave so she and Hakeem could talk, and I could get some sleep. She sent my daddy home as soon as she woke up, because she knew he worked in the morning.

I walked into the condo, took my shoes off, laid on the couch, and turned the TV on. I grabbed the house phone and dialed Zane's house number. It rang a few times before Big Mama's voice came on the other line.

"Zane?" She asked.

"No, Big Mama, it's Moet. Is Zane home?"

"Girl, I thought he was back in the city. No, he left here last night and went to a friend's party. What you need?"

"Oh nothing, just wanted to talk to him."

"You love that man, don't you?" I could tell she was smiling through the phone.

"I do, Big Mama. But I won't keep you. If you hear from him, let me know," I said, and she agreed.

I leaned back against the couch and closed my eyes for a couple minutes, before I heard the front door open and Navi walk in with a phone to her ear. I swear that woman kept a phone glued to her ear. I sat up and looked at her alarmed face.

"Moet, don't worry about it. I'm handling it," she said and turned the TV off.

I was confused about what she was talking about. I was just relaxing and now here she is telling me not to worry. That was usually when people decided to worry. I looked at my phone and realized I was getting tagged in so much stuff. I didn't bother to check my phone because my sister was most important. I clicked on some tags, and my stomach became so weak. Zane's ass was laid up on Cabrina's fake ass titties. My nose started to flare and I threw my phone at the TV, shattering it. I got off the couch and was ready to fight. Right about now, I was ready to whip Cabrina and Zane's ass.

"Just relax, Moet. I'm handling this," she assured, but I wasn't hearing none of that.

"Nah, what you need to do is book me a flight to Los Angeles right now," I said, grabbing my little bit of clothes I did have there.

"This doesn't feel right, something must be up with Zane," she came to his defense, but I wasn't hearing none of that shit.

"How many more times is he gonna do this? I let the first time slide, but now this? I can't ignore this bitch either. She knows we're together, and each time she has disrespected me!" I yelled, and pulled on my Balmain boots the stylist sent me. I was going to stomp this bitch out.

"I'm booking your flight right now. You'll have car service waiting for you," Navi told me, as I threw a bunch of shit into Zane's Louis Vuitton duffle.

"Okay, let security know I am coming down." She went to call them. Since he slid that ring on my finger, he wanted security with me at all times.

"Moet, please don't go out there and do something stupid."

"If whipping both of their asses is stupid, then call me dumb," I said swinging my bag over my shoulder. "Where's he staying? Because I spoke to Big Mama this morning and he's not there."

"He's at his condo in Hollywood. I just spoke to security there and he's still asleep." I headed downstairs and was whisked into the car, and we headed to the airport. I had dark shades on and was pissed the fuck off. I wasn't in a crying faze, it was more like I wanted to fuck shit up and then head back home.

I don't care if she drugged him, she should have never been that close to drop the drug in his drinks. I couldn't keep doing this and I *wouldn't* be doing this shit. If he wanted to be my husband, that nigga was going to go on a 'I hate Cabrina tour' right got damn now. We arrived at the airport, and I went through security and then boarded the plane. Of course, paparazzi was there.

*

I landed in LAX and car service was waiting for me. I had a hoodie on and sunglasses, so I wouldn't be recognized. Will and Jada Smith had landed, so they were focused on them, and I was able to slip into my awaiting car without being noticed. Hell, I wanted to go over there and get an autograph. I thought the flight would calm me down, but I was more enraged than ever. The condo wasn't too far, so we got there in no time. I had to keep taking deep breaths because the way I felt, anybody was liable to get it. I had a bad temper and people knew this, so why did people try me?

I got out the car, grabbed my bag and entered the building. Navi had already gave me all the information, so I headed upstairs. Soon as I stepped off the elevator, Calvin was sitting there in a chair. He got up and his eyes popped out his head.

"M…Ms. Moet," he stammered, and I put my hand on my hips.

"Save all that shit Calvin, and move your big ass out my way," I said, pushing past him.

I walked into the condo and looked around. Funny thing is, I never been told or invited here. I saw a woman's shoes, and a latex dress over the couch. I picked the dress up, and went into the kitchen and dragged a knife through the front of it, making it a coat. I laid it right back on the couch and put my bag down. A bottle of wine was cracked open, so I helped myself to a glass and walked to the back. My stomach felt so sick watching them cuddled up like they were a couple. I stood on Cabrina's side, with one arm crossed and holding my wine glass.

I lifted the wine glass, and busted her in the face with the glass. She woke up gasping and clawing at nothing in particular. Zane jumped up too, and he looked at me shocked, and then at Cabrina confused.

"B…babe?" he questioned, while still looking at Cabrina and then me. When it finally registered, and he looked at the look on my face, "W…whoa, ba…babe, I sw-" I held my hand up, not wanting to hear anymore.

Cabrina was still in the bed holding her face, and when she finally got the glass and wine out her eyes, she looked right into my eyes. "Now, on more than one occasion I told you to leave what's mine alone… Didn't I?"

"Bitch, I'm gonna fuck you up." She tried to get off the bed, but my left hook to her jaw put that at a halt.

"Who you fuckin' up? Not me, not Moet," I said, and punched her again.

Zane was in a daze, because it took him a minute before he realized what was happening and intervened. He pulled me off a screaming Cabrina, and Calvin came in and scooped me in his big ass arms, while Zane tried to get a screaming Cabrina, who was holding scissors.

"Bitch, try it! I fuckin' dare you, and we'll both be in the emergency room. You for getting your ass whipped, and me so they could remove my foot from your ass!" I screamed, trying to get free from Calvin.

"Cabrina? What the fuck are you doing here?" Zane asked. He was really trying to piece it together, but everything was happening so fast that he wasn't able to.

"I helped your drunk ass home last night, and stayed the night," she clarified, while holding the scissors with a bloody face.

"Where the fuck is Hakeem? Where the fuck was you, Cal?" he roared, looking around for answers.

"I was off last night," Cal said and held me back, because I was inching towards this bitch.

"Hakeem is by my sister's bedside. She was in an accident and he rushed to be by her side, nigga!" I yelled, and tried to get at Cabrina's fake ass.

"What? What happened to Monett?" He walked closer to me and touched my face.

"Don't worry about it, Zyair. It's obvious that your needs are being kept here," I said, and walked towards the bathroom, but backtracked and decked Cabrina in her face one last time.

"Moet, I swear I didn't even know she was lying next to me. Ma, I was knocked the fuck out and feeling sick. Last I remember is when Hakeem was chilling with me," he pleaded his case, but I wasn't trying to hear it.

"This ring obviously meant nothing when you placed it on my finger. You want your cake and to eat it too. I'm tired of this bitch," I pointed to her and screwed my face up.

"He was mine! I was there for him and handling all his needs. Then you show up and think I'm supposed to shove my feelings in my pocket and move on. No, it doesn't work like that bitch!" she screamed, and I looked at her ass unfazed.

"Nah, that's exactly what you're supposed to do. You should want more for yourself than being second, mama. But your hoe ass would rather be second. I flew halfway across the damn globe, and you're still messing with this chicken head," I said, and pulled the camera up on my phone. I took a few pics and closed my phone. "Guess who'll be laughing on the blogs tomorrow morning! Get the fuck out my condo now!" I screamed, and she didn't budge. "Cal," I said, and he gently grabbed her and showed her to the living room.

I followed her with my arms folded and watched as she looked at her dress. "This is a five-thousand-dollar dress!" she squealed, and I laughed.

"Go suck and fuck for a new one, you damn cum dumpster. Get the fuck out," I ushered her out, while Zane sat at the counter.

"This isn't even your place," she protested, and I shoved my ring in her face.

"Yes the fuck it is, and do you see the owner protesting? Nah, you don't, so go on about your business," I said, and shoved her ass out the door with Calvin. I turned my attention back to a quiet Zane. "Now you, I'm sick of this bullshit. If this is what I have to look forward to while being married to you, I don't want it," I said, pulling my ring off.

"Don't you ever take that ring off, Moet. I don't care how mad you get," he barked, and I slipped that shit right back on my finger. That didn't stop me from talking shit though.

"How you barking at me, when you had another bitch in your bed?"

"Be serious, Peanut. You think I knew that bitch was here?" he said, walking back to the bathroom and whipping his dick out and peeing.

"How I know you didn't fuck her?" I accused, and he frowned at me.

"Wanna smell my dick?" he asked, and I declined. The day I had to smell a nigga's dick was the day I would be leaving a relationship.

"Zyair, I'm not doing this with you anymore. I got on a plane and came across the damn globe. That should tell you I ain't wrapped too tight, so why you keep trying to bring that side out of me? You promised you wouldn't put me through what I been through and look," I said, holding my arms out.

"Bae, I put that on my life I didn't touch, fuck or kiss that girl. I didn't even know she was here until I felt liquid hit me in the face. I'm done with her, and I plan on letting everyone know that shit. She's not running off my name anymore, ight?"

I rolled my eyes and bypassed him. I grabbed my duffle bag and headed toward the door. "Zyair, when you are ready to make this relationship work, then come find me," I said, and walked out the door.

"What the fuck you talking about, Moet?" he yelled, but I continued down the hall. I came to Los Angles and served my purpose. I didn't need to be here any longer. I wasn't breaking up with him, but he had to know I wasn't going to go for the dumb shit. I had a flight leaving tomorrow night.

I had a few emails from this photographer for this urban magazine. He had been begging to fly me to L.A. because he said I was perfect for the cover of his magazine, but I always declined. I hit him up and set up a shoot with him. Now that I knew Monett was in good hands, I had time off from work and I had nothing to do, so I was going to do the shoot. Zane had better get in line, because I wasn't going to play these games with him.

Zane

What the fuck man? How did I end up in this bullshit, again? Cabrina's ass was relentless on fucking up what I had with Moet. She didn't care how she did it or how much damaged she would cause, but as long as me and Moet wasn't together, it would all be worth it. When I opened my eyes and spotted Moet standing there with her mean mug and a screaming Cabrina, my heart jumped out of my skin. I fought for a living and that never scared me, but Moet mean mugging me scared the shit out of me. That left hook she delivered to Cabrina's face had me wincing and jumping back, in case she decided to deliver some over my way. I was pissed the hell off that Cabrina would take it upon herself to get in my fuckin' bed. She knew Moet was my fiancée, but she still couldn't keep her distance.

I grabbed some sweats and ran downstairs, just as Moet's car was pulling away from the curb. I was pissed the hell off, as I walked back into the building. I called Hakeem's ass and he answered, laughing at whoever was in the background.

"Nigga, Moet's ass just came in my crib, beat Cabrina's ass and then left," I told him.

"What? Why the hell was Cabrina in your crib?"

"Nigga, she helped me home. You didn't tell me you were dipping. She ain't break up with a nigga, but she said I need to get my shit together."

"So get yourself together than, nigga," he laughed, and I sat on my couch.

"Why did you let me get fucked up like that?"

"You're a grown ass man, you can hold your liquor… Well I guess you can't," he laughed.

"Fuck you, Hakeem. I gotta make this up to my baby," I sighed into the phone.

"You need to do that photo shoot, and cut all business deals with Cabrina. I'm both y'all managers, but that's what needs to be done if you're really serious about Moet. Y'all still haven't officially announced the engagement."

I tapped my hand on the couch for a minute. "Ight, set that up. I think I'm gonna do my training in New York. I don't need anymore distractions, and Cali is distracting me like a muthafucka."

"I'll fly the trainer in. You know he has a home in the Hamptons, so that's not the issue. I'll set the shoot up and we'll be good. Make it right with Moet. Oh, and don't get fucked up by Moe," he joked.

"Ha, ha, real funny. She scares me, nigga. She was whipping Cabrina's ass in here, and it took Calvin to get her off him."

"So stop fuckin' with her heart. I gotta go, my baby calling me."

"Ight, give Monett my well wishes," I said, and ended the call.

I had to make shit right with my baby and do it fast, because she had a nigga low-key scared. I was going to let her calm down before trying to track her ass down. I hit Navi up, because I knew she would know.

"Mm hmm," she answered, and I was already picturing her damn face.

"What? I gotta hear it from you now?"

"Zyair, that woman smashed your television and flew across the damn country. Now, it may just be me, but she ain't fixing to play around with your ass. Why the fuck do you keep messing with Cabrina?"

I got up and walked to the balcony and took a seat on the chair. "The crazy thing is that I wasn't. Cabrina's ass was being sneaky as usual."

"Uh huh, well it ain't that sneaky because she was doing that shit on social media. Get your shit together, Zyair. If you are serious about Moet, you need to quit it, because she'll fuck you up and leave your ass. You have so much, so you need to stop jeopardizing it with hoes. Now I got to go, but you better make it up to her."

"Call her and find out where she at," I begged, and she laughed.

"I don't need to call her because I know where she's at. You're not my only boss now," she giggled.

"Moet hired you? For what?"

"Some things she was looking into doing and needed my help. I'll send you the information to where she's at," she informed me before hanging up.

I called the maid service and got dressed so I could head home. Navi sent me the address to where Moet would be tomorrow, so I put it on my schedule and headed home. I knew Big Mama would have a lot to say, since Cabrina's messy ass wanted to put pictures on social media. I gave the key to the doorman so the maid could get in, and caught car service home. My car I left at Rocky's house, was already in my garage. My phone started buzzing and I thought it was Moet, so I picked up.

"Moe?" I said, almost in a panic.

"Zyair! This took the fuckin' cake!" Cabrina screamed through my phone.

"Cabrina, didn't you learn? You ain't my fiancée's biggest fan right now. I'm done with you, and I'm engaged. Let that shit sink in, and leave me the fuck alone. Oh, and we'll have a meeting to sever any business deals we had inked together," I informed her and ended the call, as the driver pulled into the gates of my crib.

Soon as I walked through the door, Big Mama was sitting in the kitchen with her coffee, and the television on. She shook her head, as her eyes followed me through the kitchen. I hated when she silently scolded me, because the verbal scolding was to follow.

"Did I ever drop you on your damn head, Zyair? Have you been knocked around too many times? Tell me something because this foolishness you are doing is ridiculous, and embarrassing. Who is this new piece of tail?" She sipped her coffee and placed the cup down.

I hopped on the counter and looked into her hazel eyes. I could tell she was pissed, but I told her to quit watching and listening to the blogs and media. "Big Mama, nothing happened. It was a misunderstanding," I started, but she held her hand up.

"Misunderstanding my ass. You were caught right in the bed with that whore half naked. Unless you got a twin brother I don't know about, then it's all you, boy," she scolded, getting up and stirring her pot of greens and lima beans.

"What's the occasion, Big Mama?" I asked, trying to bypass all this Cabrina shit. I was caught in a bad situation and I was wrong. I should have never allowed myself to get that drunk.

"I have company staying a couple days, so I'm making dinner," she snapped, and shoved past me.

"You got a man, Big Mama?" I laughed, and she rolled her eyes.

"I have plenty of men, but it's a lady friend," she said, then started cleaning her chicken.

I looked at my phone at all the messages Cabrina's ass was sending me. She was pissing me off, but I wasn't going to give her ass any attention. I logged into my Twitter, and decided to issue a statement to clear all this shit up.

"I am happily engaged and soon to be married to the lovely @SipMoet. I was tricked and that isn't cool. I and @CabrinaTheModel aren't together and will never be, because I am going to be a happily married man soon!"

Soon as I sent the tweet, people were retweeting me and sending me direct messages. I knew Cabrina was going to be pissed, but I didn't give a damn. "Big Mama, you need more towels in your wing of the house," Moet said, coming down in a white towel, with her hair wet and dripping down her back.

"Big Mama, you're cold," I said, hopping off the counter and walking over to Moet, who had her eyes rolled so high in her head all I saw was the whites of her eyeball.

"You gonna talk to me?" I asked. Instead of responding, she sighed and walked away. I was right on her ass, following her to Big Mama's wing. I pulled her toward my wing; she protested but eventually came.

"Zyair, I'm not in the mood right now. I want to take a nap and prepare myself for tomorrow."

I continued to pull her through my wing, until we made it to my bedroom. She stood by the door and crossed her arms. Navi's little ass lied to me, and I was gonna get her ass back. "What you got planned tomorrow?"

She leaned against the door and screwed up her face. "Why you worried?"

"Because… You're my fiancée."

She unfolded her arms and slapped her thigh. "Ohhhh, so now I'm your fiancée. Nigga please," she waved me off.

"Moet, knock the shit off."

"Or else what? You gonna go lay up with Cabrina's hoe ass?"

I got up and sighed. I was rubbing my temples because this is what her father warned me about. Them damn Rubbins women had smart ass mouths. "Or else I'm gonna do this," I said, and pinned her against the wall, slipping two fingers into her wet hole. What I thought was gonna be a lovemaking session turned into something else. Moet hauled off and slapped the shit out of me, and went into my bathroom.

"Now, I bet you'll learn your lesson about touching my cookie. You don't get to be cookie monster, because you were munching on another bitch's!" she yelled, and went into my closet.

"Moe, look at me." She stopped and looked at me. "Why I got to lie? Have I ever given you a reason… Remember what we said?" I walked closer to her and she folded her arms.

"Yes, you gave me a reason prior to this. Zyair, this shit is getting old and it just started. Like come on, if I am going to be your wife, I can't do this."

I walked to her and touched her face, and bent down and placed a kiss on her lips. She moved her face and was about to slap my ass again, but I dodged her and smirked. "Peanut, I promise this is it. No more fuck ups, I promise," I tried to walk toward her, but she moved.

"Yeah, I'll believe it when I see it. I'm going to bed," she said, and walked out my room. I had slept the entire day and it was evening. I was going to make it up to her. I hopped in the shower and then laid across my bed. Before I knew it, I was out cold.

Chapter Two

Moet

The next morning, I was dressed and out the door. Matt, the photographer had arranged to have car service pick me up early. He wanted to take some pictures in the studio, and then he wanted to get some pictures of me on Rodeo Drive. He said he knew some boutique owners that wanted a couple pictures in their clothes. This was all new to me, and I probably wouldn't do it again, but I just needed something to do while being out here. Plus, Matt had been relentless about shooting with me, so I didn't want to let him down. Zane's ass thought he was slick by trying to sneak into my guestroom. I locked the door, and he knocked and whispered damn near all night. Big Mama's ass put him in check, and I didn't hear from him for the remainder of the night. I was done torturing him, but he had to know I wasn't going for his foolishness, and he had to choose. If he wanted to be with Cabrina, I would have to just respect it. But, if he wanted to be with me, he had to stop letting that bitch get so close to him. After talking to Hakeem, he did say that Zane was pretty fucked up when he left him, so Cabrina most likely used that for leverage.

We pulled up to the studio and I jumped out. Matt was waiting and smiling like I was a celebrity. "Girl, I appreciate you coming and doing this for me. Like for real," he gushed, as he pulled me inside.

"Thank you for having me, I appreciate it," I smiled, and followed as he pulled me into his little office.

"Alright, so let me tell you that I am being petty, but I shot with Cabrina a couple months ago, and without makeup, you're way prettier," he complimented, and I smiled.

"She's a pretty girl."

"I'm not saying she isn't, but you're a gorgeous girl, and I can't wait to shoot you." He waved my statement off and looked at me for a while longer. "That mess with she and Zane on the blogs, RUMORS!" he yelled and laughed.

It was nine in the morning and he was on ten. "Between you and me, it's true, but they didn't fuck. We're very much still engaged."

"That's what I am talking about hunnie! That hoe wanna ruin happy homes; well she need to go find one. Let's get you ready, doll." He pulled me to get my hair and makeup done.

After I finished getting my hair done, I couldn't stop looking at myself. My blond bundles were up in a high ponytail, and my makeup was flawlessly done. I went to wardrobe and I had on a pair of panties, with a bra and mink coat. I had so much jewelry on, I could barely stand straight.

"Bayyybay, I'm gonna need for you to serve. Like give me that 'I still got my man, and I'm still the shit' face," Matt called, and I laughed.

I put my finger to my mouth and pulled my lip a little bit. I was serving, and I wished Monett was here. She would be standing here screaming and cheering me on. We did over a million pictures in different outfits, before it was time to go to Rodeo Drive. Me and Matt rode over in his BMW truck. He already had his staff there and they were setting up.

"Mama, you killed this," he complimented, and I blushed.

"I tried, but this was more for fun for me," I admitted, and he looked over at me.

"Boo, you got a gift. You need to let me get you on some magazine covers. Karrueche and India Love are winning right now, and that little hoe, Kylie Jenner too. You need to dominate this game," he gave his opinion.

"I love them, but I'm not built for this modeling and limelight crap. I'm a nurse and content with that," I replied.

"Well, at least I'll be the one and only photographer to shoot you," he laughed, and we headed to the shoot.

We were an hour into the shoot, and the hot ass California sun was pissing me off. Plus, the paparazzi was out and shooting from behind the yellow tape Matt had set up. "Mama, I know it's annoying, but come on, serve for me," Matt coached, so I put on my good face and decided to get this shit over with.

"SIRRRR! NO CARS OVER HERE!" I heard Matt yelling.

I looked over and damn near burst out laughing. Zane's crazy ass was ghost riding his Bentley, and singing "My Place" by Nelly and Jaheim. Like, I really was hysterically laughing.

"When we laugh or we cry it's together, through the rain and the stormiest weather, we gon' still be as one it's forever, it's forever," Zane sang off key, while hanging out the car.

"Girl, is that your man?" Matt asked, and I shook my head shamefully.

This man knew how to get on my nerves, but make me laugh. I had to hide my face, because he had tears streaming down my face and messing up my makeup.

"Moet girl! You know a nigga luhhhh you!" he sang, and everyone was laughing. Paparazzi was having field day, and this crazy negro didn't give a damn. He continued to sing, as I walked over to him.

"Zyair, what are you doing?" I tried to choke back my laugh.

"You told me to find you when I was ready to make it work, and I am," he said and stopped the car. "Bae, you might wanna step back, this ghost riding the whip business is serious. That nigga E40 don't know what he talking about," he said, as he tried to hop in the car and stop it.

I laughed and watched as he finally stopped the car. He came around and looked me in my face. "I'm done, and I want you and only you. I wanna get married, have some babies and just do us. If modeling is what you wanna do, I support that shit." He pulled me into his arms.

"Modeling isn't what I want to do. I'm a nurse and I am content with that. I just did this to try it out," I told him, and he looked relived.

"You look pretty, baby," he smirked and I blushed.

"Thank you, Zyair. I need you to be serious from now on. I'm done being crazy over another bitch. You need to make me feel secure, or else I am gone," I warned him, and he pulled me into a big ass kiss. He was kissing me so hard, I thought I would pass out from all the air he was pulling from me.

Matt walked over just as he released me and smiled. "Moet, we got enough pictures so you can head out if you want. Keep my number, because I am always in New York and we can link. You are chill as hell, girl," he hugged me.

"For sure. I got a sister and she's definitely into modeling, so hit me and we'll set something up."

"It's two of you? For sure, I'll be there next week, we'll definitely link." He hugged me again and dapped Zane.

Zane opened the door for me, and I stepped in. I was still tickled by what he just pulled, but I was still a little mad about the situation. He had to let this bitch Cabrina know that I wasn't the one, and she had to step off. It was apparent that all the glass I threw in her face didn't work, so now I needed Zane to step up and the do the glass shattering. Not literally, but fugitively.

"Ma, I should have never got drunk like that where she was able to get that close to me. I apologize and I'm coming back to New York with you," he informed me, and I looked at him shocked.

"What about training and Big Mama?" I crossed my arms and looked at him.

"I can train anywhere, and Big Mama is a grown woman," he laughed and pulled off. I didn't know how he drove with all the lights flashing.

"I don't want you coming back to New York because you think that's what I want. If California is where you train at, then train here. But don't do no shit that'll have me coming back out here," I warned, and he shook his head.

"Nah, I'm gonna be in New York. I wanna be closer to Tammy and Rick right now, and you too, bae. You need to get anger management because you didn't have to bust that girl in the face."

"Yes the fuck I did, and I'll do it again. Keep trying me, Zyair," I threatened, and he held his hands up before putting them back on the wheel.

We decided to stay in California one extra day, before heading back to New York. He wanted to tell Big Mama and get his affairs in order in California, before coming back to New York with me.

Tammy

Another damn day and another mess. I threw my legs over my bed, and looked at the empty spot next to me. Lord knows I missed my husband laying next to me in bed, or even watching him get up for work. Now, he slept in the guestroom in a hospital bed, with everything he needed around him. I was his wife, nurse, home health aide and only visitor. His cancer was progressing, and with him not wanting treatment, it was probably making him worse, but he didn't show it. I had begged his doctors about giving him his treatments, but they wouldn't do it without his consent. It was fall and the holidays were coming. I wanted my husband to be here to celebrate Dion's first Halloween, Thanksgiving and Christmas. Hell, I wanted to bring in the New Year with him, too.

I slipped my feet into my slippers and made my usual rounds. I stopped into Dion's room, got her diaper changed, and put her on my hip. Then, we walked downstairs into Rick's room, where you could hear the oxygen machine before you entered the room. He was sitting up on the bed watching the news, and looked over at me with a slight smile on his face.

"Good morning, ma… How you feeling?" he asked, and reached for Dion.

I handed her to him, and sat down next to him. "I'm good, baby. I wish you would sleep in the room with me," I pouted, and he laughed.

"These machines and shit is too loud. You already taking care of me, at least you can get a good night's sleep. Plus, you know the stairs are too much for a nigga," he countered, and I rolled my eyes. "Come lay in here with me at night, and then we'll go from there," he offered, and I got excited.

"Ready for some breakfast?" I asked. He nodded his head, and I helped him up and into his wheelchair. The doctor felt it was better for him to be downstairs, since we had a lot of stairs, but I can admit I was being selfish. I wanted my damn man upstairs with me and my daughter. Damn doctors already separating us and shit.

"Tam, I'm going over to my mom's crib today," he announced, and I placed my hands on my hips.

Now, Rick's mother was a saint when it came to him and her granddaughter, but that woman couldn't stand me, and the feeling was mutual. She thought she would be able to tell me how to act, and how I should address her. Bihhh, I don't even respect my own mother and do those things, so I damn sure wasn't about to that. Plus, she always felt like I made Rick marry me. The nigga showed up at my mama's house with a ring and a key to an apartment. How the hell did I make him do it?

"Want me to drive you over there?" I asked, and he shook his head no. "Well then who's driving you?"

"My cousin is coming to get me. I know you don't like mama and she don't like you," he chuckled.

"Call Juan, Jose, or Papito and tell them I will bring you," I said, pouring his orange juice and handing him his medicine.

"Damn Tammy, that's fuckin' racist," he joked. Rick was half Puerto Rican, and I don't know why he saying I'm racist. Half those muthafuckas are named that. "Tam, your ass is already on ten all the time since finding out about this, so take some time off and relax. Mom will have Dion, and you can relax and kick it. Did Moet get back into town?" he questioned, as he took his medicine.

"I don't know, maybe you should ask her while you're joy riding with Papito." I slammed his breakfast down and ran upstairs. I heard him calling my name, but I ignored him. I was allowed to be selfish right now.

I ran into my room and slammed the door. I started pacing the floor and ranting to myself. I can admit that I am selfish as fuck when it came to Rick and his family. His family cared about only him, and some of them didn't give a fuck about Dion. My whole pregnancy, I can count on one hand how many times somebody called and checked up on me. When I had my baby shower, I didn't invite none of them bitches. Now, since everyone knows he sick, they felt that he needed to be with family. Bitch, I am his family and the one who has been doing it since I found out. The house phone rang and I answered it.

"Yeah," I sat on the edge of the bed and looked for my blunt; it had become a daily little habit for me.

"Hey, it's Blake."

I looked at my phone like I had seen the devil, and he was trying to square up with me. This bitch had a big ass pair of balls. "Blake, I ought to beat yo' a-"

"Listen, I didn't call for all that. I just want to meet with you and talk. We get into fights all the time, and I wouldn't be a true friend if I didn't reach out to you," she said, sounding all sincere and shit.

"What the hell we need to meet for?"

"I…I just need to really speak to you about something. Can we meet at Juniors downtown?"

I sighed, and looked at the time. "What time?"

"A little after two."

"I'll be there. Oh and Blake, if this is some shit, that ass whipping I put on your ass, this time it'll be ten times worse," I let her know, and she agreed.

I composed myself and went back downstairs. Rick had finished breakfast, cleaned his plate and had Dion in her bouncer in front of the TV. "You done tripping?" he asked, as he looked in the freezer.

Although he had to be in the wheelchair to prevent falls, that didn't stop him from cooking dinner and still doing things around the house. Except now, he got tired and by the end of the day, he would be exhausted.

"Yep, I actually have plans of my own," I smirked, and took the pack of meat he took out to thaw.

"Oh yeah, with who?"

"Ricardo, do I be in your business?" I walked past him, but he pulled me on to his lap, and rolled us into the guestroom.

"Hell fuckin' yeah you do."

I rolled my eyes and crossed my legs, while looking in his eyes. "Rick, I want another baby before you go. It'll be just me and Dion," I pouted. I had been thinking a lot of about this, and I didn't want it to be just me and Dion when he left this earth.

"If you're serious, we can do this," he said, like it was no sweat off his back.

"How Rick? You been through so much radiation, your sperm is gone."

"When I first found out, I knew it would be selfish of me to start this treatment and not put my jimmy's up for when you wanted another baby. All we have to do is call the doctor, and set that up," he explained, and I smiled.

"You were doing a lot of sneaky shit, Rick. I wanna get pregnant as soon as possible," I said, like this was the answer to our problem. In reality, my child probably wouldn't be able to meet its father. But, right now it felt like the solution to all our problems.

"We can make that happen, ma," he assured me, and I was excited.

"Can you consider going on treatment again? For me and Dion, and our future child?" I batted my eyelashes at him, and he gave me a serious look.

"Tam, all that chemo and shit was making me fuckin' sick. I haven't vomited, been feeling dizzy or anything. That shit is poison and it hasn't been doing anything. Only thing I need, and that's when I'm sleeping is my oxygen machine; all that other shit is bull."

"Come on, Rick. I know Big Mama used to do this holistic medicine when she had her breast cancer a couple years back. If I find out what she did and stuff, will you do it?"

"As long as that shit don't make me sick," he agreed, and we kissed. "Now, get your ass on the bed and spread those legs," he demanded, and I got on the bed ready to be dicked down from my husband.

*

I found a parking spot a block away and walked to the restaurant. Once Rick's cousin picked him and Dion up, I decided to pull myself out my sex coma and get myself together. For a nigga with cancer, he still got that dope dick. I walked into the restaurant, and saw Blake already sitting down. She kept looking between the menu and her cell phone. I slipped into the booth and looked at her. I didn't want any food, and I damn sure didn't plan to stay long. I told Monett I would take her to the hospital. She had been home a week, and was complaining about pain and bleeding. Hakeem was out of town on business, so I agreed to take her.

"Thanks for coming, Tammy," she started, and I looked at her. What did she want me to say? You're welcome, oh and how is your face after I fucked you up?

"What did you need to meet me about, Blake?" I tapped my fingers on the table.

"I'm pregnant and Ki won't answer his phone or even acknowledge me when he does see me."

"Now, what the hell does that have to do with me, Blake?"

"As a friend, I thought you would be there for me. I plan to keep this baby," she said, sounding so damn stupid.

"I heard you were fucking his brothers too, so it could be any of theirs. You need to just do what you think is best. As an ex friend, I'm telling you not to call me again. You do shit that you know is fucked up and don't care about the repercussions. Now you are sitting here pregnant with God knows who baby, and the damn daddies are avoiding you. Karma is a bitch and she'll get you, and it looks like she got you," I stated, and grabbed my bag and left the restaurant. I don't know why she thought I would have some kind of compassion for her ass. She fucked my best friend's man, and then had the nerve to fuck his brother unprotected, which ended up with her getting pregnant.

As I was walking back to my car, I bumped into a lady. I excused myself and continued to my car, mad that I even agreed to come over this way for Blake's ass. "So you can't even say hello to your mother?" I heard the woman say. I stopped in my tracks and turned around.

I looked at the woman, and it was surely my mother. She looked like she gained weight, and appeared healthy, but that was how it always started. "Hello, Tonya," I dryly replied.

"Damn Tamala, you have to be this cold? I've been calling your phone about seeing my granddaughter." She walked closer to me and I moved back.

"What do you want? I have things to do and unlike you, I keep my word."

"I fucked up, but I am clean now. I'm taking it one day at a time, but I am clean, Tammy," she tried to convince me, but I wasn't hearing it. How many times is she going to come in my life screaming she's clean, then go back and do the same thing.

"How many times have you done this, Tonya? I'm not putting my daughter through that, I know that for damn sure." I turned and continued slowly to my car.

"I heard about Rick…." her voice cracked, as it trailed off.

"DON'T!" I yelled, but realized I looked crazy. "Don't you talk about my husband," I scolded, pointing my finger. This time I turned around and hurried to my car. I blamed Blake for this bullshit. If I didn't know better, I would say it was planned. But Blake knew nothing about my mother and her drug problems. I started my car and headed to Monett's house to take her to the doctor.

Monett

I know y'all probably think I'm stupid for not telling everyone who was responsible for the accident. I knew I probably should, but I just didn't want to right now. It was too much drama for me right now, and I didn't want to deal with it. Me and my son were fine, so that's all that matters, right? I waited outside my parents' house for Tammy, and when I saw her round the corner, I walked down the stairs. Since yesterday I had been having bad cramps and spotting. That wasn't what concerned me; it was the heavy amounts this morning I found. My mother was with her sisters and my father was at work, so I called Tammy to take me. She popped the locks and I eased in, wincing in pain.

"Damn, what the hell happened from the day you were released to now?" Tammy asked, as she pulled away from the curb.

"I was cramping, but this morning I was bleeding like crazy."

"Oh Lord, let me get you to this hospital. Where is Moe?" she asked, and I looked up from my cell phone.

"She and Zane been held up in their condo since coming back. I don't want to keep bothering her anyway," I waved it off, and Tammy pursed her lips at me.

"Girl, don't be hating that Moe finally getting her some. Once you drop that baby, you'll get you some too," she joked, and I laughed through the pain I was feeling.

Once we made it to the hospital, we went through check-in before we were sent to an exam room. The doctor came in and did an ultrasound and pelvic exam. I noticed while he was doing the ultrasound, he kept looking at the screen with a worried expression.

"Is anything wrong?" I asked, startling him.

He exited out the screen and wiped my stomach off. "Uhh, give me a minute to get my attending," he said, and rushed out the room.

Both me and Tammy looked at each other and shrugged our shoulders. I was a little worried because of the doctor's facial expression. A couple minutes later, the doctor came back in with another doctor.

"Hello, Ms. Rubbins, can you lay back for me again?" he asked, and I laid back. Again, they put that cold ass gel on me and he moved it around, while paying close attention to the screen. I could never really tell what was on the screen, but when they showed me my son's penis, I saw that clear as day.

"Is everything alright?" I questioned, getting irritated. I saw Tammy tapping her foot, so I knew she was ready to go off already.

"Ms. Rubbins, you have a placenta abruption and we need to schedule an emergency C-section now," he informed me, and turned to the other doctor and gave him instructions on what to do.

I sat up in a panic. "Is my baby alright?"

"The heart beat is getting slower, so we need to hurry. As of right now, your baby is fine, but we need to move," he encouraged, as the nurses and aides came in and took the brakes off the bed I was sitting on.

"I'll call your parents and Moe; do you want me to call Johnathan?" she asked, as they wheeled me out the room.

"Yes, please," I said, as I tried to breathe in and out to calm myself. They took me straight to the operation room, and got me prepped for this C-section. I hadn't had time to tell Tammy to call Hakeem.

"Lean up, baby girl," the anesthesiologist said, as he inserted the epidural in my back. I winced in pain, and wished I wasn't alone. I looked up, and Tammy was standing on the other side of the door, waiting for them to allow her in. I smiled, because no matter what, our family could always count on Tammy's crazy ass.

They laid me back and got the setup together, and Tammy came in and sat on the stool next to me. "It's going to be alright, suga." She tried to make me feel better, but I was scared.

"I hope so," I sighed.

"Now Monett, you're going to feel a lot of pressure." I heard a familiar voice and it was my regular doctor.

"How-"

"I was working in here today, and I heard about a placenta abruption, and I knew it couldn't be anybody but that stubborn baby boy you're carrying," he laughed. "Let's get this baby into his mama's arms, people." He winked at me and started to cut me. "You're going to feel a lot of pressure," he warned.

I closed my eyes and thought of all the good times I had with Johnathan, and all the positive things. I really didn't want anything bad to happen to my baby. "Moe and your parents are on their way. I called Johnathan, and he's on his way too," Tammy informed me, and kissed my forehead.

"Thank you, Tammy."

"I wouldn't miss my nephew coming into this world for nothing."

We heard crying and tears came to my eyes, as I heard my son's first cries. The doctor held up my light-skinned baby boy and I burst out in tears. He looked so much like me when I was a baby, and I couldn't stop crying. They took him over to clean him up, and Tammy followed, snapping pictures. They brought him over to me and I put my face to his, and smiled. He had a little Johnathan in him, but he was all me.

"Hi baby boy… I'm your mommy. I love your little butt so much," I kissed him, as the nurse took him.

"He's still considered premature, so we're taking him to NICU so we can check him out," the nurse said, as she placed him in an incubator and took him out the operation room.

"Let's get you stitched up so you can join your baby boy," my doctor said, smiling.

I leaned back and let out a breath of relief. I was happy that he was alright, and I didn't have too much to worry about. "Monett, he is a big baby. He's seven pounds and you're only eight months. Dion's ass was like six pounds and I was over my due date, her frail ass," Tammy laughed, and I joined in with her. She knew how to lighten the mood for sure. I was happy that my son was alright.

*

After getting stitched back up, I was sent to recovery where I fell asleep from the ride back from the operation room to recovery. I was out for a good while because when I opened my eyes, everyone was in my room. My parents were the first to run to my side, and Moe got off Zane's lap and tried to climb in the bed with me.

"I'm so sorry baby girl," my dad apologized like it was his fault.

"Daddy, it's fine. Where is my baby?" I asked, looking around at everyone.

"He's in the nursery, Monett. He's fine and you're fine. Get some rest and we'll take you to see him tomorrow," my mother patted my hand while looking at me.

"You're a mommy, Monett. He's so cute, and looks just like you… I love you, boo," Moet said with tears in her eyes.

"Stop crying," I said and looked for Tammy, but she was gone. "Where is Tammy?"

"She headed home to be with Rick and Dion. She told me she'll be up tomorrow to see you," my father informed me and I nodded.

The door opened and Jonathan walked in. My father pursed his lips up, because he couldn't stand Johnathan. He still didn't know that I was in an abusive relationship with him. Plus, nobody knows why or how I got into that accident, and if they knew it was Jonathan, he would be in the next hospital room.

"Sorry I'm late, I work in Jersey now," he said, and stepped closer to me.

"Can y'all give us a minute please?" I looked at everyone, and they filed out the room. Moet looked at him with a deadly grin.

"Moe," I said, trying to hold in my laugh. My sister was a damn demon in disguise, but she protected her family, and it didn't play when it came to us.

He pulled a chair up to me and sat down. "I guess you didn't tell your family what happened," he started.

"Not yet."

"I want to apologize to you, Monett. I have an alcohol problem, and I've known for a while but have been in denial. My father went through the same thing and I grew up watching him drink and beat the shit out my mother. Imagine my surprise when I'm walking in the same footsteps." He sighed and reached for my hand. I allowed him to hold my hand. I did love this man once upon a time. Although he put me through hell, my heart wouldn't allow me to harm him the way he did me.

"Johnathan, you could have killed me or our son. This drinking has to stop," I said, wiping my tears. The thought that he could have killed me and his son kept flashing in my head.

"Monett, I am getting help and I'll be going away to a live in rehab center. AA meetings aren't going to help me. I want to be in my son's life," he said, and I could tell he was holding back his tears.

"Even after all you put me through, I will never keep your son away from you. Get yourself right and we'll be right here waiting," I touched his shoulder.

"You will?" he looked shocked.

"Meaning, I will be here with your son. You'll always have that relationship with your son."

"What abou-"

"We're done, Johnathan. I'm happy and in a relationship right now with an amazing man. He makes me feel on top of the world, and like the luckiest girl in the world. I wouldn't give that up for a second chance at a disaster," I tried to say gently, but the smile that came across my face whenever I spoke of Hakeem was enough to light up a whole room.

He looked sad, but he nodded his head. "I feel you, Monett. Can I see my son?"

"Go on in the nursery and tell them who you are. Good luck, Johnathan," I said, and he bent down and hugged me.

He left the room and Moet was the first to enter. She climbed in the bed with me, careful not to hurt me. "What was that about, Monett?"

"Nothing, he wants to see his son. Why there always gotta be something extra, Moet?"

"Humph, because I know you like to hide shit. But, if that's what you're sticking to then fine."

"Yep, did you take a picture of him?"

"Uh huh." She handed me the cell phone, and my heart melted. My son was so beautiful, and resembled me so much. I couldn't wait to hold him and count his little toes and fingers. "What you gonna name him? I have a few," she snickered.

"Girl, you aren't naming my child. But his name is Nautica Richard Rubbins," I stated proudly, and she laughed.

"My nephew will not be named Nautica. He'll get picked on like crazy, Monett."

"Yes he will. I've been sitting on that name for a while. Nauti for short," I explained.

"Umm, I guess so. Have you called Hakeem?"

"No, I forgot to tell Tammy, and I'm sure she doesn't have his number."

"Oh, well I'll give you some time to rest and call your boo. I'm gonna take mommy and daddy home, and I'll be back up with some food and a change of clothes." She kissed me and left out the door.

I was finally able to sit back and close my eyes for a minute. I grabbed my cell phone and dialed Hakeem's number. He answered on the first ring, like he always did.

"What's good, baby? I've been calling you all day," he answered, sounding worried.

"I had the baby," I revealed, offering a weak smile like he could see me.

"W…what? Are you serious, Monett?" he stuttered.

"Yes, his placenta had separated, so we had to rush and do a C-section. He's fine and I'm fine, so don't worry."

"Ma, how can I not worry? You had your damn stomach ripped open and I wasn't there. Were you alone?" He spat his questions one after another.

"Tammy was with me until my parents and Moet arrived. Baby, I am fine, and you don't need to rush and be with me. I'm fine," I assured, but he wasn't trying to hear me.

"I'm heading home now."

"Hakeem! You're not going to keep pushing things and canceling things because of me. I am fine, and can wait until you come home. Now, when were you suppose to return back to New York?" I raised my voice a little.

I didn't want him to keep putting off his duties as a manager, to keep running to my side. I'm a big girl and can handle mostly everything that is thrown at me. "I'm supposed to be home in two days," he sighed.

"I'll be getting released in two days, so I'll see you then. I'll be staying at my parents' house until we get a place, okay?"

"Sounds like the best idea. Ma, let me get back to this meeting. I'll Face time you tonight," he assured me, and we ended the call.

I laid back down and decided to get some sleep, because I was going to be up bright-eyed and bushy tail to see my baby boy.

Moet

I looked through Monett's closet, as Zane sat on the bed making comments about how fat my ass was looking. I ignored him and continued packing some of Monett's stuff. For baby Nauti, she had his bag already packed, so I didn't have to worry about that. I felt Zane's hand caressing my ass as I dug into her bottom drawer for panties.

"Zyair, if you don't quit," I threatened, and saw him smirking in the mirror.

"You got them leggings on and got me wanting to do some things to you." He licked his lips and palmed my ass.

"Boy, please move so we can go back to the hospital."

"Nah, you still need to be in your room and pack your stuff," he demanded, and I looked at him sideways.

"I'm not moving in yet."

"Moet, I don't have time to play with your ass. You got a whole closet in our crib, and if you gonna be my wife, you're gonna be in that condo. Fuck you thought, I'm gonna be in that bitch alone? I get scared and need that big ass booty to rub on," he joked, and I rolled my eyes.

He got up and left the room, so I continued grabbing things I knew Monett would need. When I looked in the hallway, Zane had some of my clothes from my closet, into the hall. "Zane, what the hell are you doing?"

"I told ya ass I was serious. I'm tired and I only moved this much. I'll have the movers over here tomorrow." He brushed me off like it wasn't a big deal.

"I can't with your hardheaded ass," I sighed and crossed my arms.

"Yet, you marrying a nigga." He kissed me on the cheek and handed me the keys to his Benz. "I gotta run and handle something real quick."

"Big headed ass," I mumbled.

"Fat booty and crusty toes," he yelled back.

I laughed and replied, "My toes cute!"

"Yeah, ight," he hollered back, and closed the door. I wondered what he had to handle, but I let it pass my mind. I didn't want to question him, so I focused back on getting Monett her stuff.

I passed my mama, who was sitting on the phone with her sisters. My mother didn't have friends, but my aunts were her world. "Mama, I'm going to drop this off to Monett, and then I'm heading to Zane's house," I informed her, and she placed her hand over the phone.

"From what I hear, it's y'all house," she snickered.

"Please mama," I rolled my eyes and laughed.

"I'm just saying. That man gets your feisty ass in shape." She laughed and went back to talking on the phone.

I kissed her forehead and packed Monett and Nauti's stuff into the backseat. Since Monett totaled my car, I didn't have one. I was either being driven around, or he had me driving his cars. I didn't mind because I liked to be chauffeured around. I had become quite spoiled, but when it was back to work, I was driving my own whip. I hopped into the car and pulled off toward the hospital. I looked at my ringing cell phone, and it was Tammy.

"What's up, mama?" I greeted. We didn't have much time to speak, because she was rushing out to go pick Rick and Dion up.

"Would I go to jail if I punched Rick's mama in the face?" she asked without a hint of laughter in her voice.

"Tammy, you cannot go around punching people's mamas. What happened?"

"She trying to move into my shit, and Rick is considering the shit. Hell nah, I like having my peace. Just me, Rick and my baby girl. I don't need her telling me how I need to care for my husband."

"Tam, I'm not taking her side but you know how you get. You shut everyone out and we don't hear from you in days. His mama probably be worried and wants to spend as much time as possible. You should allow her that time," I advised and she sucked her teeth.

"She better get a room down the block. She's not living in my shit, because I don't need the stress in my household. Next thing I know she's throwing fiestas in my shit, and talking about me in Spanish," she vented, and I had to laugh.

"Now you know Rick's mama speaks English and if she gonna curse you out it's going to be in English. It's your home so do what works, but allow that woman to visit her son."

"Now that I can do, but anything else, she's tripping."

"You so damn crazy. Where's my God daughter?"

"Sleeping, her greedy ass. Now, the real reason I am calling is because somebody has a birthday coming up."

I laughed and rolled my eyes. I hated and loved birthdays. I hated them because I was getting older and loved them because it was all about me. "Yeah, I know. I have no clue what I am doing… probably dinner and some shopping."

"Uh huh, well let me know what you're doing so I can make sure I get a sitter," she told me, and we ended the call.

I arrived at the hospital and walked into Monett's room. She was sitting in the bed with Nauti right in her arms. She looked so peaceful laying there with her son. The glow on her face couldn't be described. It was an aura about pregnant women, or new moms that made them look beautiful. The fact that they just had given birth to another life, made me look at them like super heroes. Well, my big sister was a super woman, and so was my mother.

"Thank you," she whispered, taking him off her nipple.

"You're welcome," I quietly said, and walked over to her side and kissed his head. "He's so beautiful, Monett," I cooed, looking at his little handsome face.

"I know, I made the nurse bring him in here. He's all mine." She kissed his face and I sat down and crossed my legs.

"What's going on with you and Zane?" she questioned as she burped him. It was like she was a natural.

"After I popped up on his ass, he's been good. This Cabrina chick is really wrapped into him. Like damn bitch, move the hell on," I sighed, and let my hair out my ponytail.

"Whatever they had, had to be more. She's acting like they were married or something. He better put that in a smash, quick." She looked at me rubbing my tracks. "It's time to get those taken out and redone," she advised.

"Don't I know it. I'm trying to think what I'm gonna do to it."

"I need mommy to set up my room with the stuff from the baby shower. I'll call her tomorrow and ask her."

I yawned and stretched my arms. "I'll do it, don't worry. I'm about to go to Zane's and I'll be back tomorrow before work. They trying to make me take time off for your accident, but I need the money."

"Alright, love you Moe," she said, and I kissed her and my nephew before I headed to Zane's house.

I had been at Zane's house for two hours and his ass still hadn't dragged himself through that door. I was sitting in the middle of the bed with my hair all wild, and I didn't care. My hair needed to breath and that shit was itching. Once I washed my hair and conditioned it, it would be nice and curly and I could sport a ponytail. I wasn't a bald bitch, and didn't wear weave because I had to. My phone rang and I jumped off the bed to answer it. I sucked my teeth when I realized it was Ki. I had been ignoring him since he called me a couple nights ago. I didn't want to hear anything he had to say. We were as good as done and he knew that. So why bother to call?

"Yes, Ki?" I answered, sitting down on the edge of the bed.

"Moe, can we talk? Before we were together, we were friends. You can give me that much," he said, sounding desperate.

I sighed and crossed my legs. He was right; before anything we were good friends. However, it was hard being friends with someone you couldn't trust. I didn't owe him shit, but the Libra in me wouldn't allow myself to end the call.

"What's up?"

"What's up with us, Moe? We've never gone this long without picking up the phone and speaking. Can you come through my office tomorrow so we can talk?" I hesitated a bit because I didn't know where things would lead. I also was in a relationship, and I didn't want to disrespect Zane.

Throwing caution into the wind, I decided to meet him. "Yeah, I'll come through on my lunch break. It's nothing really to speak about, but I'll hear you out. Night Ki," I said.

"Night Moe," He replied, and I heard him say I love you, but I acted like I didn't hear him.

I sat on the edge of the bed for a little while with my phone in my hand. I didn't know what to say or do. I knew for sure I didn't want to be with Ki, but why was it so hard to let him know that? This nigga fucked my friend and continued to be with her behind my back. Yeah, we weren't together, but she was the reason I went the fuck off on him and he continues to fuck her.

"What the fuck? You got in a fight, bae?" Zane asked, kicking off his sneakers and sitting next to me. He started to pick through my shit, and I slapped his hands.

"Why you always snapping jokes? My shit good," I laughed and got off the bed, but he pulled me onto his lap.

"That's because I love you. You still love me, ma?" He looked at me and I shrugged my shoulder.

"Sometimes, depends on what you do."

"Damn, I can't express my love to my woman?" He pushed me off his lap, and I fell on the floor and laughed.

"Zyair, don't get fucked up. Let me get in the shower so I can be ready for work tomorrow." I sucked my teeth and he laughed.

"I'd like to see you try. You hungry?" He picked his phone up and I nodded my head.

"Get me some Boston Market with a sparkling lemon lime water from Walgreens down the street!" I yelled my orders from the shower.

I heard him call me greedy, but I continued to wash my hair with my mind on Ki. It was like every time I was happy, he would come and try to fuck it up. But, being the person I was, I couldn't allow myself to be happy unless he was too. Fucked up right? Don't I know it.

"Ma, I sent the order out with Calvin. He'll be back soon," he yelled, undressing and jumping in the shower with me.

Before I could even reply to his statement, I felt his hands all over me and his lips on my neck. I let a moan escape my lips because whenever he touched me, my body automatically opened up for him. He knew how to make my body cream without having to do much. He slipped his fingers inside of me and I held the walls. I knew this man was about to have me screaming his name with his cocky ass, but I would scream it anyway because that's how he made me feel.

"Uhmmm, babyyy th…the food," I moaned, and he continued to suck on my neck as he played with my goodies.

"Don't worry 'bout that. You'll eat, but right after I get some desert first," he said, and pushed me over to the stone bench. He lifted one of my legs over his shoulder, and put his lips on my lips. He was flicking his tongue over my pearl, and I was squirming and screaming.

He pressed down with his thumb, while he flicked his tongue a few times, and I thought I died three times. I was breathing all hard and trying to catch my breath, but just when I did, he did something else. The entire bathroom was filled with him slurping my juices. It sounded like he was slurping the juices from a clam at dinner time.

"You ready for some dick, smart ass?" he smirked, and picked my ass up and held me up on him. I was waiting to see beads of sweat or a sign of struggle, but my man held me up, as he slammed into me.

When I tell you I died three times and God brought me back, I ain't lying. He was really digging my back out. "Yesss, yeshhhh, ughhh! Zyy…airrrr… I caantt, I cannn," I moaned, while scratching his back up.

"You can't what? Got your ass sounding like the little engine that could." He put me down and turned me around, and slipped right inside of me. He had his hands tightly gripping my hips, as he crashed himself into me.

I gripped the wall as I came and was shaking, but he didn't care, because he continued to dig deeper. I felt him tighten up, as he released himself into me. We washed each other up and got into the bed. Calvin's ass came an hour later, but I was cool because I got my food and was watching my reruns.

"Damn, this shit good… Too bad I gotta stop eating like this." He shoved some mac and cheese into his mouth.

"I'll continue to eat like this for you," I laughed, and he pushed me.

"Greedy ass. But for real, I wanna take you out to dinner tomorrow night so come straight home," he revealed and I smiled.

"Oh yeah? What's the occasion?"

"I wanna show my fiancée off and make her feel good. Don't need an occasion for that."

"Let me find out," I smirked, and handed him the empty container of food and laid back.

My body was sore and I was full. That was enough for me to take my ass to sleep. "Night baby, I know your ass 'bout to be knocked." He reached over and kissed me on the lips, and I closed my eyes.

*

From the time I walked into the work until now, I hadn't had a sip of water or a seat. Tanisha's ass was handing off all her patients because she claimed she wasn't feeling well. If my memory served me correctly, that was what the fuck sick time was for. She pissed me off to the fullest, but I stayed away. I loved my job and didn't want her ugly ass to be the reason I lost it.

"Girl, I feel like my ass is about to fall out," she randomly said, as I was about to stick my teeth into my sandwich. I placed my sandwich down and looked at her nasty ass.

"Maybe you should go home. Use your sick or personal hours," I reminded her, just in case she forgot.

"I used all those up with my man. He took me to Puerto Rico last week, and now I think I am paying for it," she continued to tell me, like I cared.

As long as I've worked here and had to deal with Tanisha, we've never had a conversation, or at least a civil one. She was the queen of shade, but when it came to pettiness, she didn't stand a chance. However, it was a little refreshing not to be arguing or getting ready to place her head through a wall.

"Maybe it was something you ate while you were there," I suggested, and she shook her head.

"You're probably right. I may need to get myself checked out too. I've been feeling like this since I returned."

"You should do that. I'll take over here," I offered, and she agreed.

"Thanks Moet. Oh, and how's your sister? I heard she came in, but I was on another floor."

"She's good, just had the baby. She should be getting released tomorrow."

"Oh okay. Congrats," she wished, and walked down the hall crunched over and holding her ass.

On cue, it was Ki calling about our talk we were supposed to have. I closed my sandwich because my appetite was ruined from

Tanisha, and answered my phone. "Ki, sorry I can't meet you, but you can tell me now while we're on the phone."

"Damn Moe. You really can't come and speak to me? It'll be quick I promise."

"Ki, I don't have the pleasure of working for myself like you do. I have a shift to do, and I am currently covering someone else's too."

"Can I come through there really quick?"

"Sure, but I can't talk long, so make it quick."

"Bet," he ended the call, and I went to handling files, and tossed my sandwich away.

Thirty minutes later, Ki came strolling from the elevator and smiled when he saw me. It was sad that I no longer got those butterflies I once did when we were together. Men didn't know a good thing until it's gone, and then they want to whine and cry about how they were getting it together. Nah nigga, you should have been had it together.

"Can you cover for me really quick?" I asked my other co-worker, and she agreed.

I grabbed his hand and led him to the cafeteria. We sat a table near the window and I looked at him blankly. I remember it was a time when I worshipped the ground this man walked on. Now, I didn't even want to have this talk. I was so far done that he didn't need to further explain shit to me. It didn't even matter to me anymore.

"Moe, I want you and I'm changed. I'm done with those chicks and have you worrying about me. Baby, I swear you have all of me. All I'm worried about is my business and you. Remember, I still got the condo for us." He reached for my hand, but I gently took my hand back.

"Ki, you don't know how long I wanted that to happen. I wanted you to always choose me and leave those other chicks alone. You're too late and I always told you that you would say this." I ran my hand through my curly hair. I was rocking it curly, and I loved it; but, I knew I needed to get my weave in to protect my hair.

"You in love with him, huh?"

"I am, and I'm going to be his wife pretty soon. He makes me so happy, and he has his faults, but the way he makes me feel outweighs all of that," I explained, thinking of my baby. Yeah, he was acting up and Cabrina was in his bed, but once I got the full story I believed him.

"This shit doesn't have nothing to do with that nigga, Zane. You ready to be living up in that big ass crib and shit, that's all," he implied, and I rolled my eyes.

"I'm already in that crib and I'm still at work. I don't care about his wealth or fame. Wouldn't I be doing all these photo shoots I'm offered daily? That's not my life and you know that. But, a broken hearted nigga will say anything. Later Ki." I got up and went back to work. I didn't have time to go back and forth with my past. He was my past for a damn reason.

Zane: Miss you ma

Me: I miss you too. I'll be working late tonight. Srry

Zane: Damn. It's cool

Me: Love u

Zane: Love u too

I placed my phone back in my pocket and went back to work. I didn't know what Ki expected me to do. Call off my engagement for a nigga that didn't give a fuck about me or my feelings? I had work to do and didn't have time to be trying to rehash the past with Ki. He better find Blake and move the hell on, because I am.

Chapter Three

Zane

I placed my phone in the passenger seat as I sped through the city. Today I declined any car service and security. Calvin's ass was my roll dog, but he was on thin ice. He needed a few days to get his shit together, before I sent his ass packing back to Cali to become a bouncer. Yesterday, Hakeem had me running around doing a million things for him and Monett. He wanted to surprise her, and had me running around doing it. I passed it on to Navi, but she made my ass go along with her. Now, I was going into a meeting with my lawyers about cutting ties with Cabrina. Since Moet got in her ass, she still was calling my phone and begging me to come back to California to be with her.

I blocked her ass and planned to get my number changed, but I had a lot of people that had this number. If her ass continued, I was gonna have Moet's ass handle her again. That situation she put me in was fucked up, and I shouldn't have expected nothing less from Cabrina. The valet took my car and I walked into the building and went up to the desired floor. Soon as I stepped off the elevator, my lawyer was waiting for me. I walked into the room and wanted to walk right back out. Of course, Cabrina's ass would make it a point to fly all the way to New York for this meeting.

Any other meeting we had regarding lawyers, her ass could never make, but this one she wanted to show up at. I sat down and told the assistant to get me some water. She hurried to fulfill my request. As I looked down at my cell phone and replied to emails, Navi walked into the room and sat beside me. I smiled, because she knew how to be there for a nigga without me having to ask.

"Mr. Whitfield, I understand that you want to breech all contracts you have regarding my client," Cabrina's lawyer stated.

Nick, my lawyer, didn't bother to look at me before he replied. "That's exactly what he wants. We're even prepared to pay the companies to avoid being sued."

Taking a sip of his coffee, Cabrina's lawyer said, "Even my client? I mean, she is missing out on money from this irrational decision your client is making."

"My client has been harassed and assaulted by your client. It's safe to say that their business dealings need to come to an end."

Cabrina was rolling her eyes and scrolling on her phone, unbothered. "Listen, I have a fiancée and Cabrina isn't making it easy to work with her. Each function she is coming on to me, and it's making my fiancée uncomfortable and honestly, the contracts aren't worth the stress I will have to deal with going home. I'll give Cabrina ten thousand dollars so we can end this thing." I leaned up in my seat and wrote my number on a paper, and slid it across to her.

She uncrossed her legs and pulled herself closer to the table. "Ten thousand dollars when I would be making over sixty thousand dollars from these contracts? Please, Zyair. All of this over some pussy!" she yelled.

"If we're stating facts, you would only be making that money off of the Zane Whitfield name, not your own. We're not trying to stop you from fulfilling your contract with these businesses. But, Mr. Whitfield's name will be coming off all promotional flyers used to promote the products or events," Nick explained.

"You know without your name they will drop me, or get a whole bunch of reality stars to host and market these products," she whined, looking into my eyes. I guess she was looking for a glimmer of hope, but there was none.

"The only reason I did half this shit was because of you. I don't need to host and promote products. I'm a fuckin' millionaire. I make money in my sleep; you need this, not me."

"When that bitch runs you dry you'll be begging to do these appearances."

"If she runs me dry, we'll be good because she has a career. But she's not into that materialistic shit like you, Cabrina. Can we sign some papers?"

"We'll be accepting the ten thousand dollars as well," her lawyer spoke up.

"That deal isn't valid any longer," he smirked, as Cabrina dotted her I's.

"Ughh! I hate him! I hate him!" she cried in the office, as I dipped out the office.

"Nick, my man! That's why I pay you all that money," I dapped him, and he assured me everything will be good, and to let him know if she's using the promo material with my name, and we'll sue the shit out of her.

Me and Navi walked out the building and I held the door open for her, as the paparazzi snapped pictures. I hopped in the driver's side and pulled off.

"I can't stand that chick. How she thinks she'll continue to live off your name while trying ruin your life?" She sucked her teeth and shook her head.

"Cabrina ain't nothing but a gold digger, and I'm glad that her ass got the hint. She'll be heading back to California and I'll be here in New York."

"Congrats on getting this handled. Take these papers and celebrate. I still have to finish doing the last minute run around before Hakeem gets into town." She looked through her cell phone, and jotted a couple things down.

"I'm gonna send him your bill, because that nigga's using you more than me," I laughed, and she waved me off.

"I don't mind, you know, since you don't have much work for me."

"Man, I can hand you all this shit I've been holding. I'm gonna need you to find us a private gym. Plus, I need my whips sent here, and find me a barber out here… The list goes on," I told her, and watched as she wrote down the things I needed.

"I'll have that done for you, boss," she smirked, as I pulled up to her condo.

"Kiss my niece for me," I said, as we hugged and I pulled off. I had something special planned for my baby tonight. I headed home to get shit right for tonight.

I could have easily had Navi pull off what I was trying to do, but then it wouldn't be special. Since she was working late, I planned to have a nice dinner and a bath waiting for her. Then, I was going to show her the papers from earlier. I still had to plan what I was doing for her birthday. I had no clue what she wanted, so I called my cousin. I hadn't caught up with her in a minute, so I wanted to see how she was.

"What do you want, big head?" she answered, and I laughed.

"I wanna see how my fam doing over there," I replied, and she sucked her teeth.

"Rick's doing pretty good, but he's still losing weight and doesn't have an appetite. His mother comes over here every damn morning trying to feed him all these different soups she done researched."

"Damn, you need to give that nigga some weed. It'll help him with eating; you know once a nigga take a pull he'll have the munchies," I joked, but she didn't laugh.

"You know what, let me call you back, Zyair," she started, but I stopped her.

"Nah, I called for a reason and I ain't hanging up until I get that answer," I protested, and then heard the sound the iPhone makes when someone hangs up on you.

I sat there for a minute before my phone started ringing again. "Yeah," I said.

"My bad, I had to call you from my cell phone," she explained, and sounded like she was walking. I could hear the wind blowing in the phone.

"Where the hell you going?"

"Hold on, again. Aye, where's Dread sheisty ass?" she said in the background.

"What you need?" I heard the person reply, and then Tammy came back on the line.

"Ugh, I hate buying weed from these boys. But you're right, I can give Rick's ass some. But what you need help with?"

All I could do is laugh at my cousin's crazy ass. Only she would run out the house to cop some weed for her husband. I heard the door close, and I assumed she was back home. "Moet's birthday is coming; what you think I should do?"

"I just called her big headed ass and asked the same question. She claimed she didn't know and would probably keep it simple."

"Only she would want to be simple on her birthday. I'm thinking of throwing it a club… What you think?"

"Eh, I think it has been done so many times already. Take her away for a vacation or something; she'll like that," she advised, and I nodded.

"That nigga still owes me a trip," I heard Rick's big ass mouth in the background.

"Tell that nigga to sit his ass down and I got him!" I yelled back, laughing.

"Uh huh, hopefully it ain't my ashes, nigga," he replied and we both laughed, but not Tammy.

"I don't find that shit funny, Ricardo. Get your ass out my face before I push your ass down," she scolded and turned her attention back to me on the phone. "Now, take her away and spoil her. Make sure you request the time off from her job, too. You know how that girl gets with her job."

"You right, I got something planned. I'll let you know when it's in stone."

"Alright, love you." We ended the call and I got back to cooking.

*

I heard the elevator open and Moet on the phone with her sister. They were talking about the baby. She placed her work bag and purse on the counter and sat in the chair. She didn't even see the layout I had in the dining room. I waited until she finished her conversation to sneak up behind her, and sneak a kiss.

"You scared me… What you doing, weirdo?" she kissed me on the lips, as I took her arms and pulled her to the dining room.

"Since we couldn't make dinner, I wanted to bring it to you. I know it seems like the odds have been stacked against us, but I want to reassure you that we're good and we're going to make it down the aisle to the altar," I whispered in her ear, and she held the side of my face.

"This is so sweet, baby. I love this and you so much," she squealed and stood, taking in the view.

I had the shades pulled up so the city was our background. I had the table set with a bucket of Moët on ice. The plates were set, and all I had to do was serve our food. I called Big Mama a few times to help me cook. I was sure this food was gonna be good, so I wasn't worried. I pressed the stereo and "The One" by Tamar Braxton came on. This was Moet's favorite song.

"I don't want nobody else. Baby, all I need is you. You're the one I want," she sang, as I held her chair out. I watched her round ass sit down, and I pushed her in. "You really showing out, huh?" She bobbed her head to the music, as I filled her flute up with Moët.

"This isn't showing out. I wanna make my woman happy and make up for my fuck ups, so this is me being a good fiancé." I kissed her on the cheek, and went to the kitchen.

I made steak, potatoes, asparagus and corn bread. I plated her food and set it down in front of her, and she looked at me shocked. "You made this, baby?"

"I know how to cook a little. I do my thing in the kitchen, don't look so surprised," I joked, and sat down and poured myself some Moët.

I looked into her eyes and she looked into mine. This moment felt so good and right. The lights were low, and the candles were lit. Dru Hill "These Are the Times" was now playing softly as we looked into each other's eyes, not saying a word. I could see the feelings she had for me in her eyes. I could also see the hurt that she still felt, and I was determined to get all of that out of her. I never wanted my future wife to hurt because of me or anybody else. I wanted her to always be happy. Going to bed angry with each other wasn't an option. When I'm committed to her, there was no divorce. We were going to make it work, and be everything to each other.

I handed her the papers from earlier and she looked at me strangely before opening them and reading it. "What's this, Zyair?"

I reached for her hand and caressed her small hands in mine. "I wanna make it right between us, and I couldn't as long as I was holding on to something. Today, I went to a meeting and ended all my business deals with Cabrina. I don't have to see her, work with her or speak to her," I announced proudly.

"When I said that I was mad, I didn't mean that. I don't want you to give up on money because of me and my insecurities. You said nothing happened, and I believe you," she touched my hand.

"Moe, it's not healthy for us if I continue to break bread with her. She wants us not to work and that doesn't work for me. If she can't respect my relationship, regardless of what we had in the past, I can't be around her. I didn't need that money, and I only did it for her."

"If you're happy about this, then I guess I am," she smiled, shoving some potatoes into her mouth.

I cut into my steak and added some of the rosemary and garlic butter I made. Big Mama was telling me all her secrets, and I added them to dinner. "I am. Plus, I'd rather be in business with my future wife."

"Oh no, I am not doing business with you. I am content with my job. We haven't talked about the wedding and a date. Or is the engagement still valid now that you decided to keep your butt in New York?"

"Peanut, I'm marrying your ass. Whether you like it or not," I smirked, and she smiled.

"Well, I want to be your wife, so I'm happy about that."

Big Mama's voice came into my head, and I knew it was time to bring up the subject of a prenuptial agreement. It didn't matter how much I loved Moet, because I had a family and myself to protect. Don't get me wrong, if something happened and we broke up, I would never leave her with nothing. She was my wife at one point, so she'll always be straight.

"Baby, we need to talk about some thing," I started, and she sipped her drink then looked at me.

"Okay, let's talk." She set her fork down and paid full attention to me.

I never got tongue tied or nervous, but with Moet's beautiful big eyes staring at me innocently, I felt bad. "We need to sign some papers before getting married, bae."

"I know, you want me to sign a prenup, right?" She returned back to eating her food.

"Yeah, how you feel about that?"

"I would never try and take what wasn't mine before I entered the marriage. But, I know you need to look out for your family and your money. Emotions run high during a divorce, so you want to be protected. That doesn't make me feel differently about you. It makes me love you more."

"For real?" I asked, choking on my drink.

"Yes, you're thinking of your family first. Although we won't be getting divorced, I love that you are thinking about your family. I'll sign the papers, Zyair," she giggled, and took our plates and set them on the counter.

She came back and sat on my lap, kissing me on the lips. "I love you, you know that?" I kissed her on the lips.

"I know that. Whenever you want to meet with your lawyers to sign those papers, just let me know."

"I'm gonna leave you straight too, you hear me?"

"I don't need that. If we get divorced, we'll go our separate ways with what we came into the marriage with. I don't need your money or support."

Damn, where did this woman come from? Any other chick would be in a full argument with me over this, but Moet didn't seem bothered by it. Despite what she said, I was going to leave her off financially set. She was stubborn and would deny it, but I was gonna add that clause after she signed.

"I got a bath running for you in the bathroom. Go get undressed and get in, and I'll be right behind you," I disclosed, and she smiled.

She got up and headed to the back, and I went to get the cut strawberries, chocolate and whipped cream I had prepared earlier. The strawberries were all cut up sloppily, but it was an E for effort, right? When I walked into the bathroom, she had a glass of wine while sitting in the bubble bath.

"You knew exactly what I needed, baby," she moaned, as she laid her head back.

I sat on the edge of the tub and rubbed a strawberry in chocolate, and she opened her mouth as I placed it in. She took a bite and chewed slowly. "I'm glad that I could make your day less stressful." I kissed her on the lips and she held on to my face.

"Thank you, baby. But those strawberries are big as hell," she giggled and splashed me. I continued to feed her strawberries and wine, as we talked about any and everything. It didn't always have to be sex with us.

*

I woke up with Moet laying right in my arms. She was knocked out and snoring. I quietly moved out the bed, and picked up her ringing cell phone. That shit been going off all morning, and she could sleep through anything, so I knew she didn't hear it.

"Hello?" I answered, walking into our master bathroom to handle my morning business.

"Can I speak to Moet?" I heard a male's voice. I looked at the phone and the number wasn't even stored. The fact that another nigga had the nerve to hit my girl's phone had me already pissed.

"Who the fuck is this?" I looked at myself in the mirror. I needed a fresh line up ASAP.

"Ki, this her man?"

"For you to ask that question means you already know the answer. Fuck you need to speak to her about? Y'all done, you need more explanation?"

"Yeah, that's what you think, but I just saw shorty yesterday. You wondering why she came home late, huh? Cute ass Mickey Mouse scrubs she was rocking yesterday, ass real fat in those pants too," he added, but I wasn't gonna let that nigga see me sweat.

"Your point is what though? You second, because she came home to me… A nigga like me don't got time to play these little kids games. I think that's why Moet left your ass, because you couldn't pick one toy to play with, you had to have them all… selfish nigga," I chuckled, and ended the call.

I didn't need to question Moet about where she was. I knew she was at work and I trusted her. I also knew that nigga was just like Cabrina, trying to fuck up a happy home. I continued to get myself straight for today. Hakeem's plane landed in an hour, and I told him I would pick him up. I dressed in a pair of Distressed jeans with Timberland boots and a cashmere sweater, and a pea coat. I kissed Moet on the cheek and headed out. She needed to get her rest because she worked tonight.

Pulling up to the airport, I watched as Hakeem hurried to the car. He threw his shit in the back and hopped in. "What's good, nigga?" We dapped hands, and I sped off.

"Good, good, handling business. I heard about the business shit. Cabrina called me crying and shit," he revealed and I laughed.

"She wants you to talk to me?"

"You know she does, but I told her it wasn't my business. I gotta find that girl something to do. Between me and you, her career ain't hitting right now. With y'all break up and shit, nobody throwing offers out like before. That new chick India loves hitting the scene with The Game, and shit's been being thrown at her left and right."

"That's because she was riding off my name. I'm not gonna front, it was a good marketing idea, but with me about to be married, it ain't gonna fly."

"I told her she needs to start fucking some rappers or something," he laughed, and I chuckled right along with him.

"Nigga, she got bomb head, so I'm sure they can center a reality show around that."

"Hold on, this her right now." I watched as he carried his conversation and could see the frustration in his face. Cabrina's ass was annoying when she didn't get her way, so I knew she was making Hakeem's life a living hell.

"You good?" I asked, soon as he ended his call.

"Nah, she's taking a role on that *Hollywood Ex* show. Her friend pulled some strings and she's going to take it."

I shook my head; I kind of knew she would do some shit like this, so I wasn't surprised. "What can we do about this?"

"Shit, ain't shit we can do about it. I mean, we can put a gag order or request she doesn't speak about you on the show."

"Shit, I don't want my name attached to anything she's got going on, for real," I sighed, as we pulled up to his condo.

He closed on it last night, thanks to Navi. She knew some people and she went right in and threw his offer on the table and closed. Since the building was brand new, a lot of the furniture was new and used for staging, and she managed to get them to include it in the deal as well.

"I'll handle it, but right now I need to go surprise my baby… Let me go shower real quick," he insisted, and looked around for the master bedroom. "This shit nice," he whistled and I laughed.

I pulled my phone out and sent Moet a good morning text.

Good morning baby, see you later. I sat and waited for Hakeem to finish, and thought about Cabrina and this bullshit she was trying to pull. I had to figure out a way for this shit to be stopped.

Monett

Three days and me and my baby was ready to head home. My mother and father had an appointment for my mom, so they couldn't see me home. Moet's ass wasn't answering her phone, and Tammy had an appointment with Rick. I wasn't angry that everyone had something to do because that was life. I knew how to get home with my baby. Nauti passed all the test and was cleared to come home. God didn't know how thankful I was for him getting us this far. Lord knows the odds were stacked against us, but we were going home today and that was all that mattered. Johnathan entered his rehab program, and his parents wanted to see Nauti. I told him I had to think about it. Nine times out of ten, they would have to travel to me if they wanted to see my baby.

"Come back in a week so we can remove those staples, and Nautica has an appointment with the pediatrician in two days. If you have any problems don't hesitate to come in." The doctor smiled, and handed me my discharge papers. My regular doctor wasn't here, but I wasn't tripping. Long as this man handed me my walking papers, I was good.

"Thanks, Doctor," I smiled, as I got into the wheelchair with Nauti's car seat on my lap. I was grateful that Moet brought his car seat up here or else I would be screwed.

The nurse wheeled me through the halls and outside of the hospital. She called me a cab, but this white BMW truck blocked the cab. I started to get out and curse the person out, but Hakeem walked around the car and my face lit up. I tried to get up, but the painful reminder of my incision reminded me.

"Baby, what are you doing here?" I squealed, with a huge smile on my face.

He bent down and kissed me on the lips, and looked in the carrier. "Damn, he looks just like you, ma," he said, and placed a kiss on Nauti's forehead.

"Everybody keeps saying that… Now what are you doing here?"

"I wouldn't miss this for the world. But, what kind of man would I be if I didn't give my girl a push present," he said, and pointed to the car.

The nurse squealed like she just was given the gift. I forgot she was there until her ass squealed in my ear. "What? For me?"

"Ma, you need a car to get around with the baby, and I want to know y'all are safe at all times."

My damn hormones had my soft ass crying and dripping tears onto Nauti's face. What did I do to deserve a man like this? A man that cared about me and my son. A man that constantly cut his shit short to make sure I was always good. It made going through hell with Johnathan so worth it, because it was a rainbow at the end of the tunnel, and that was Hakeem.

"Ms. Rubbins, congratulations again, and please be sure to come in if you or baby are having any issues," the nurse reminded me, and helped me out the chair, as Hakeem held the car seat.

"Thank you again," I said, and grabbed Hakeem's hand as he helped me into the front seat. I was out of breath and in pain from the staples. I didn't know how I was going to get home with just me and Nauti.

After he strapped Nauti in, he hopped in the driver's side and pulled off slowly. "Babe, you didn't have to do this," I said, holding his hand.

"I know I didn't have to, but I wanted to," he smiled at me with his beautiful smile.

"I'm so sore and in pain. I can't wait to get into my bed and lay down." I smiled just thinking of my bed.

"Uh huh," Hakeem agreed, and continued paying attention to the road.

I noticed he didn't take the exit to my mother's house. "Babe, this is taking us to Manhattan," I warned him, but he just squeezed my hand and carried on with his conversation.

One thing about Hakeem was that he was always on the phone handling business. Since we started dating I've learned to deal with it, but now I was sitting here feeling a certain type of way that he was taking a call sitting next to me. Maybe it was the hormones, but I didn't like that shit.

"I gotta make a stop real quick," he informed me, and I rolled my eyes. Damn, why the hell was I acting like this? This man just got me a nice ass white BMW truck and I was having a fit because he was taking calls in my face. The more I tried to make reason with myself, I still felt the same way.

"Sure." He looked at me, but didn't say anything else. He just continued to drive, and I listened to the music.

We pulled up to a building and he helped us out the car, as the valet driver took the car. I was confused and a little pissed. I could have waited in the car. "Where are we going? I'm in pain, Hakeem," I whined.

"I gotta handle some business real quick. Y'all can wait in the waiting office." We got into the elevator and I was pissed.

"Why the fuck your business couldn't wait? I'm bringing my son home, which is a special day for me. I don't expect you to care because he isn't your son, but it matters to me!" I yelled, pointing my fingers in his face.

"Chill the fuck out, Monett!" he hollered, making Nauti fussy.

"See what you did, dumb ass," I muttered, and snatched the car seat.

He had a tight grip on the car seat, so I gave up. We walked down the hall and he opened the door. "What kind of meeting is this?" I smacked my gums, but he ignored me.

We stepped inside and the condo was beautiful. It wasn't over the top, but it was gorgeous. Floor to ceiling windows, with a little terrace off the kitchen area. It wasn't overly large, but enough for a few chairs and a little grill. The living room was set in earth tones with a sectional, coffee table and flat screen TV on the wall. The kitchen, living room and dining room was all in ear's reach. It was open concept, which I liked.

"This is our new home. All that fussing and fighting and all I wanted to do was show you our new home," he explained, and placed Nauti down.

I could tell my words in the elevator made him feel some type of way. "Really? I'm so-"

"I'll be back, I got some business to handle," he cut me off and left out the apartment. I felt like shit for saying what I said.

I took Nauti out his car seat and walked around the condo. I went into the kitchen and it was fully stocked with food and my favorite pregnancy foods. I rocked my son in my arms, as I slowly walked around the condo. There were three bedrooms and two baths. I looked in the first room down the hall and assumed it was Hakeem's office. His desk and boxes and everything was scattered all over the floor. I closed the door, and walked down the hall and opened the door and smiled.

It was my baby's nursery; it was set up in an 'under the sea' theme. He had a beautiful silver crib with an octopus' blanket set. His chair in the corner for feedings was blue, and the rug on the floor was too. The Ashton Martin stroller Zane got me for my baby shower was assembled, along with the 4moms bouncer that he got me. I had diapers, bottles and anything you could need stocked in this room. I changed my baby's diaper and swaddled him up, before putting him in the bouncer and setting the motion for low. His little butt got cozy and went to sleep, and I went to the room down the hallway. It had double doors, so I knew it was our bedroom.

I opened the door, and the burgundy and beige color scheme he had going on was sexy. There was big king sized canopy bed with huge pillows and a comfortable comforter set on it. The room was big compared to the one I had at my parents' house. It had a bathroom with a Jacuzzi and stand-in shower. I noticed on the left side of the bed, he had a bassinet for Nauti. I dialed his number but it went to voicemail, so I gave up and called Moet.

"What's up Monett?" she yawned into the phone.

"Hakeem got me a new car, and we have a place together now. A condo on the upper east side," I blurted, and she laughed.

"Why do you sound more worried than happy?"

I sighed, and collapsed on the chaise lounge that was one the bed. "Because I was getting irritated because he wouldn't tell me where we were going. He kept saying he had to handle business, and I accused him of not caring about Nautica."

"Damn, Monett. Why the hell would you do that?"

"I know; my emotions are running wild right now. I can't control the tears," I said breaking into a sob.

"Calm down. You're entitled; you just had a baby and those feelings are normal. You need to apologize whenever he comes in. You can't keep throwing stuff like that in his face since he's not Nautica's father. In my opinion, he should have been, but it ain't my business. Where the hell is Johnathan? He ain't come help you to a new condo," she voiced her opinion.

Although I was the big sister, I felt like Moet sometimes got those roles confused. She always had me feeling like I was her little sister. "He's going through some personal issues. I told him to get himself together, and we'll be here."

"Personal issues? Bitch, please. You make it so easy for him, Monett."

"How? By saying his son will be here when he handles his issues? I don't want to keep my son from his father and I damn sure don't want to confuse my son by letting him think Hakeem is his father, because he's not."

"You're going to do what you want. I'm just saying you're making it too easy for him. But I got work in a few, so I'll call you later."

"Yeah, I guess," I uttered and ended the call.

I went to check on Nauti, and dragged his bouncer into the living room and turned on some TV. I went into the kitchen and decided to cook for Hakeem. I wanted to apologize to him, and let him know how I was feeling. That statement I made wasn't fair to him, and he had to know I was sorry.

*

I heard the front door open and close and listened to the footsteps, and doors open and close. I was in bed with my kindle, catching up on some good reads. When one of the bedroom doors opened and Hakeem appeared, I offered him a slight smile. He took his coat and boots off and went into the walk-in closet that we both shared.

"Can we talk?" I winced, as I tried to sit up.

"About?" he called from the closet, and went into the bathroom.

I walked behind him, and watched as he undressed. I just delivered a baby, and I was wet as hell and ready to climb his pole. "Uh… I just wanted to apologize for what I said earlier. I didn't mean it and I have a lot of emotions swarming around, and usually I'm good at keeping them controlled, but with these hormones they are coming full force," I explained, as I wiped the tears coming down my face.

"Cool," he replied, and got into the shower.

I was crying, and all he could say was cool? I opened the glass door and looked at him. "I'm sorry, Hakeem. I said, sorry!" I yelled through tears, and he continued to wash up like a hormonal bitch wasn't interrupting his shower.

"Ight."

I slammed the bathroom door and walked to the front where Nauti's diaper bag was. I went into his room and grabbed him out the crib and placed him in the carrier. I cried the entire time, and mumbled things to myself. I grabbed a few bottles out the fridge and left out the door. I didn't have much here, so I didn't need to grab anything other than my son and his things. I made my way downstairs and hopped in the first town car, and told them Zane and Moet's address. I apologized and that was supposed to make it better, but yet he was giving me the cold shoulder.

I paid the driver and lugged the carrier up to the security booth. They called up to Zane and he met me downstairs in a hurry. "What the hell, Monett?" He looked at me confused, and took the carrier and diaper bag.

"I'm done with Hakeem, and don't tell him where I am. Where's my sister?" I ordered, and he looked at me.

"She's at work."

"Forgot about that," I mumbled, as we stepped off the elevator straight into his condo. "We'll stay a few nights until I go back to my parents' house."

"Monett, that nigga got a whole condo for y'all to enjoy and you going back to your mama's house… For what?"

"I said some thi-"

"I know what you said. Keem's my nigga, you don't think he wouldn't vent to me?"

"I apologized and he's still giving me the cold shoulder. Obviously he doesn't want me there, so I did him a favor." I took my jacket off and picked up my son.

"You're being dramatic. Didn't they open your stomach or some shit? You shouldn't even be up doing this much."

"Women have babies everyday. I can walk and still get the hell away from someone who doesn't want to be with me. We'll sleep on the couch," I offered, and he nodded his head.

"There are enough bedrooms for y'all to sleep in. Come on so you can get some rest." He showed me to my bedroom and I got in and cuddled with Nauti.

"Don't you tell him where I am," I warned, and he waved me off and closed the door.

I nodded off and woke up to Hakeem sitting in the corner of the room looking at me. "Thanks big mouth," I mumbled, and sat up.

"Don't do shit like that, you hear me? Don't fuckin' leave out the house with a new baby and not tell me!" he screamed and stood up. "Don't do no fuckin' shit like that again, Monett!"

He was screaming so loud that Zane came into the room. "Y'all good?" he asked, wiping his eyes.

"Please get him out my room," I begged. I was scared, and holding my baby so close to me.

"I ain't going no fuckin' where. She takes the baby and herself and leaves me clueless. I didn't know what the fuck happened to her. She could have got in an accident or something. I don't do childish shit like that, man!" he yelled, and I heard his voice cracking.

"She's good, bruh. She took car service over here," Zane tried to calm him down.

"I don't give a fuck if she asked Aladdin to bring her. You don't do shit like that when you're grown!" He slammed his hand on the wall.

"Grown? You're the one ignoring me, but we're suppose to be grown, right?" I yelled back. I was tired of him throwing a fit.

"I never ignored you. You want me to accept the apology and go back to kissing your ass and it doesn't work like that. I accepted your apology, now let me get over the foul shit you said. People are allowed to feel a way!" he yelled back.

"Y'all buggin'… Come on, Hakeem. She's good tonight. You don't have to worry," Zane assured him, and pulled him out the room.

I started to feed Nauti, and calm myself down. He came in here yelling at me about where I take my son. Once I put him back to sleep, I laid down and closed my eyes again. Since coming home, it has been nothing but drama. I needed some calm to balance out all the negative that had been thrown at me.

*

I woke up and my baby was gone. I looked on the floor, under the bed and behind the bed. I started to panic, until I heard

Moe talking baby talk. I calmed down and handled my morning business before I left the room. The cook had breakfast laid out, while Zane read the paper and Moet bounced around with Nauti.

"Good morning," I mumbled, and helped myself to some eggs, toast and bacon.

Moet looked at me and shook her head. I already knew she was going to have a lot to say, but I didn't want to hear it. I was grown and I wasn't telling her how to live her life, so she needed to have the same respect.

"What is going on?" she asked, waiting for me to sit down.

"Nothing. I'm straight."

"So why are you here? Last I spoke to you, you said you were going to apologize." She burped Nauti and laid him on her chest.

"He didn't want to hear it, so I'm here. I'm tired of talking about it." I ate my food, and waved her off.

"I swear you need to stop being childish. He's not Johnathan."

I slammed my hand on the table, and Zane looked up from his paper. "Stop bringing up fuckin' Johnathan for everything. You're right, he isn't Johnathan!" I yelled.

"Alright, calm down. Damn baby been hearing more of his mama yelling than anything else since he's been home," Zane interjected.

"Listen, I just don't want you to mess up what you have because you keep thinking of your past."

"Moe, I'm not thinking about Johnathan. I left because he wasn't trying to hear anything I was saying," I shot back, and she put her hands up in surrender.

"Whatever Monett. I don't have time to be trying to figure this shit out." She got up and handed me, Nauti.

When I finished eating, I got dressed and got ready to leave. Moet and Zane were in their room, and from the noise they were making, he was breaking her back in. I got a town car back to the condo I shared with Hakeem. Whether I wanted to admit it or not, I was being childish when I left. I had to stop running from stuff and start facing them. I planned to call Moet later on because I should have never come at her like that. All she was trying to do was be a sister and I bit her head off because of it.

When I walked back into the house, it was quiet, and I could hear the television from the bedroom on. I quickly got my son into some new clothes and laid him down to sleep. I should have never taken him out last night. Once he was laying down, I went into the kitchen and washed the dishes I made from cooking dinner. I had a habit of cleaning whenever I was upset, anxious or nervous.

"Finally brought your ass home," Hakeem said, coming into the kitchen.

He had on a pair of boxers on and a wife beater. If I wasn't pissed at him I would be licking my lips, but he was on my shit list. "Yep. I'll stay out your way."

"Monett, stop being like that. What you mad for? You didn't have that foul shit said to you." He walked up closer and I rolled my eyes.

While wiping down the counter, I sucked my teeth. "Hakeem, I apologized, so if you gonna keep bringing it up I can go back to my parents' house."

"I accept your apology." He sat on the stool and I brushed past him, but he grabbed me in his arms. "Stop running away from shit, Monett. Just because you didn't get your way doesn't mean you get to grab Nauti and leave. You're not playing fair," he told me, and I nodded.

"I'd rather just leave before things escalate," I responded, and he shook his head.

"As a couple, we're going to fight, but what means more is if we can fix it. How can someone fix something if the other person is gone? Nauti isn't my son, but I'm in his life and I don't appreciate you throwing that I am not his father in my face. As much as I don't respect his father, I'd never disrespect their relationship as father and son."

Ugh, this is why I was so into this man right here. He always said the right things that made you feel better. Yeah, I was childish as hell when I packed up and left in the middle of the night, but that was how I was and I don't think I'll ever change.

"I'm dramatic, laugh at sad movies and snore in my sleep. I'll pick a fight if I'm bored, but I am loyal and love hard. I can try and do things your way, but I am who I am and I can't change that."

He kissed me on the lips and pulled me close to him. "I don't expect you to change, but I expect you to give us a chance before you throw in the towel."

I kissed his lips back and replied, "I can do that… You hungry?"

"Hook me up with something while I grab Nauti; he's crying."

"I don't expect you to take any responsibility for Nauti. I'll do it all," I called to him, and he turned around.

"That's the shit I'm talking about. I live here and I'm with you, so I'm not gonna ignore him like he's not here." He turned and went into Nauti's room.

I smirked, and went to fix him something to eat. I really needed to stop distancing him from Nauti. Just because he wasn't his father didn't mean he couldn't do for him and still actively be in his life.

Tammy

These hormones shots were pissing me off, and I didn't know how I felt about anything. All I ever did was cry about Rick and the fact that we were going through the process of trying to have another baby that he wouldn't be here to raise. Each time the thought hit my mind, I started crying like a big ass baby. I had been taking these shots for a week and thankfully, this was my last one before they went to retrieve the eggs to cook them up with Rick's sperm. I had been snapping on any and everything lately. Hell yeah I was angry that I was going to be raising my children alone. I was mad that my husband might not even make it to see our child born. I watched the other couples when we went to our appointments, with envy. I would gladly trade having another child for my husband's life.

I stabbed the needle into my thigh and threw away the stuff in the protected containers. Now that Dion was six months, I let her go with Rick's mother more. She was crawling around my house and tearing shit up. Plus, that gave me some time to spend with Rick when he wasn't sleeping. He couldn't eat, so I went and got him some weed and now all his ass did was eat everything in sight.

"Tammy, where you at?" I heard Moet call me, as she walked through the door.

She promised she was coming after work, so I was prepared for our little girl time. I slipped my feet into a pair of Uggs and grabbed my purse. Rick was in his bed with everything he needed, so I wasn't worried.

"Baby, I'm heading out for a little while with Moet. If you need me, call my cell phone," I advised, and kissed him on the lips.

I walked into the kitchen where Moet was sitting on the counter, eating some of the cookies I baked earlier. "You know those are weed cookies right?"

She spat them into her hand, and jumped down to wash her mouth out. "Is there a meth lab in the back too?" she yelled, as she continued to rinse her mouth out.

"Calm down, your ass ain't even finish it. Let's go before we lose our reservations," I rushed her, and she dabbed her face with the napkin.

"You lucky I'm hungry or else I'd be suing your ass," she joked and hugged me.

We made our way to the Bentley and I stopped and looked at her. "What the hell you doing with Zyair's car?"

"Umm, earth to Tammy; Monett totaled my car."

"Damn, I forgot about that. Shit, my mind been on so much. I'm surprised he let you drive it, 'cause your ass can't drive," I giggled, and she slapped my ass.

"Says the bitch with road rage."

We got into the car and pulled off towards the restaurant. We managed to get reservations at Nobu. It was my favorite restaurant, and I only went when Zyair's ass was in town. I looked over at Moet who seemed to be in deep thought.

"What's on your mind, Moe?" I touched her arm and she smiled at me.

"The shit with Zane's ex is still bothering me. I still picture them together in the bed," she disclosed, and I screwed my face up.

Before this Rick thing, me and Moet caught up daily. It was nothing happening without the other knowing. But now my time was spent on being there and caring for my husband, so I didn't catch up with her as much as I wanted. But with best friends, you could keep out of touch for a while and then pick back up like nothing happened.

"I read what happened, but I never asked you about it because I didn't want to upset you."

She turned down the radio, so I knew she was about to spill the tea. After she filled me in on all that happened, I had to pull my sunglasses out and sit in the car silently. "Tammy, you play entirely too damn much," she laughed and snatched the sunglasses.

"Girl, we need to start making time to catch up because that's some bullshit. So, what the hell did you do?"

"After I beat her ass, I left him and went to Big Mama's house. I told him I don't have time to be playing games with him and his ex. If he wants her, I will gladly step to the side and let them be together."

"I swear I always questioned if that boy was adopted," I sighed.

"So, he went and cut all ties with her business wise. We'll see if that works. He claims he got something to talk about when I get home." She ran her hand through her hair and sighed.

"Listen, you my girl and I'm gonna give it to you straight; Zy is a good man and he means well, but if he's stressing you out, you need to let it go," I lightly touched her arm.

We were just pulling up to the restaurant. The valet took the car and we both walked inside hand in hand. Once we were seated, the waitress came over with a bright smile and annoying voice.

"Welcome to Nobu Nyc; can I offer you some beverages?"

"I'll take a white wine, and a Grey Goose soda," Moet ordered, and the waitress turned her attention to me.

"Water with lime, please."

I knew Moet's nosey ass was about to question me. She knew I loved a drink like the next person, but with this whole IVF thing, I couldn't drink. "You pregnant?" she smirked.

"No, but we're trying. I'm doing IVF," I revealed.

She put her hand over her mouth. "Wow, are you sure you want to do this?"

"I…I mean yeah, because I don't want it to be just me and Dion. But, then I'm thinking of the emotional side. Do I really want to raise two babies without Rick?"

"I mean, be optimistic, Tam-"

"He's going to die, Moet. I have to stop looking online for different miracle cures and deal with the fact that my husband is sick and dying," I bluntly stated, and she accepted the drink from the waitress.

She took a long gulp of her Grey Goose soda before she joined back into our conversation. "I know; I just wish there was something to keep him here longer. You know, make him not sick anymore." She looked down at her cup.

"Hey, let's not talk about that. This is our girls' night and your birthday is tomorrow," I changed the subject.

"Oh, so that's why you damn near harassed me to come over," she giggled, and guzzled the rest of her drink.

"You know I had to take my boo out for a pre birthday turn up." We clinked glasses and laughed.

"Zane wants me to sign a prenup," she blurted, and sipped her wine.

Now, I was conflicted with that situation. Zyair was my family and of course I wanted him to protect himself from anything that could happen in the future. Then, Moet was my girl and I wanted her to be straight if they were to ever get divorced. I wanted her to be financially secured.

"Well, how do you feel about it?"

"I'm cool with it; I told him I would sign it, but he claimed that he was adding something where I would get something, but I told him he didn't need to."

"Moet, don't be crazy now. You deserve at least something."

"I'm leaving as I came. I'm still going to continue to work and have my own. I don't want to speak of divorcing because I want my parents' kind of love. Sleep on the couch and wake up to breakfast," she laughed, but I could tell she was serious.

"Girl, don't we all." We ordered our food and continued talking.

"So, I ran into my mother some time back. Blake's ass called me to meet her, and my dumb ass went. The girl started off with a sob story and I left."

"Humph, everything that is happening is what she deserves. You wasted your time even going to see her… Did she reimburse you gas money?"

"I ain't even worried about her ass. I bumped into my mother walking out, and she's talking about she's clean and wants to come around her grandchild. Then when she mentioned Rick's name, I went off," I ran down the story to her.

"What is wrong with people? How does she even know about Rick?"

"Big Mama's big mouth. I told her to stop speaking to my mother about my life. She didn't care to be in it, so she don't need to know about it."

"It's only right, but I appreciate you coming and taking me out, babes," she smiled and reached for my hand.

"No matter what I got going on, I'll make time for my boo." We clinked glasses again. We continued to catch up and eat, while I let Moet have as many drinks as she wanted. I planned to drive her home, and then catch a cab back home. Her birthday was tomorrow, so it was her world.

Zane

It was my baby's birthday, and she was up getting ready for work. I was trying to get a quickie, but she was complaining about me letting her sleep late. I watched, as she brushed her teeth and tried to put her hair in a ponytail all at the same time. I laughed because I had a surprise for her. I walked into the bathroom and handed her a card. She took the card and placed it on the sink, and continued getting herself together.

"Come on, Moe, open the card," I demanded, and she stopped fixing her hair and opened the card.

She sat down on the couch in the bathroom and read the card. Her breathing quickened and she looked at me and at the card again. "Zyair, please tell me you didn't," she said lowly, but I could tell she was excited and trying to contain it.

"Happy birthday, Peanut," I said, and sat down next to her.

She jumped up from the couch and started pacing the floor, while clenching the card and the contents inside. "I can't believe this, Zane!" She jumped up and down with a huge smile on her face.

"Go pack some stuff and we'll buy some stuff when we get there," I told her, and she looked at me sideways. She looked back at the tickets and her face lit up.

"We're leaving in two hours? 'Wayment, these aren't real tickets… These say Z&M Airlines," she examined, and I smiled.

I had designed fake airline tickets, since we were flying private. Z&M Airlines was Zyair and Moet Airlines. I just wanted to do something to make her smile, and make her first birthday with me special.

"Baby, I know you like to scrapbook, so I did it so you can put it in the one you're making of us," I replied, and she hugged me around the neck, standing on her toes. She placed a kiss on my lips, and started kissing me all over.

"Umm, the destination is real, right?" She stopped and looked at me and I nodded my head yes. "Babe, I always wanted to go to Amsterdam. We're going to have so much fun," she squealed and ran out the room to pack.

"I know, it was either there or Paris, but I'll save that for our honeymoon."

"Damn, I need to call in and use my personal time." She sucked her teeth, and grabbed her phone.

"Ma, I did all that, you're straight. We'll be in Amsterdam for a whole week with no interruptions. Just me and you," I grabbed her into my arms and kissed her lips.

"Hmm, I like the way that sounds, babe. This is the best birthday, ever!" She kissed me and hugged me tightly.

After calling her sister and Tammy and bragging about her birthday getaway, she finally finished packing. I told her to pack lightly, but that was like talking to a wall. I grabbed her bags and we exited the building, but was stopped.

"Aye, what's the hold up?" I asked security, since the car wasn't there yet.

"Babe, calm down; I'm sure there is a reason for it," Moet calmed me down.

We watched as the red Range Rover pulled in front of us, and she nodded her head in approval. "Happy Birthday, Moe!" I said, handing her the keys to the truck.

"What? Are you serious?" She jumped up and down as the paparazzi caught pictures of us. Calvin smiled because he knew my whole act was bullshit just to trick Moet.

"Baby, it's all yours. You keep complaining about getting to work and now you have your own whip… Drive us to the air hanger," I smiled and hugged her.

She jumped right in the car and sped right into traffic. "Baby, you didn't have to do all of this. The trip was enough, but the car… I'm going to have to go all out for your birthday."

"I didn't do it for that, Peanut. I want it to be special for you and you're going to be my wife soon. I wanna spoil what is mine," I grabbed her hand, as we headed to the air hanger.

We arrived at the air hanger and the jet was sitting there looking all pretty. Everybody was waiting on us. I had someone there waiting to take Moet's truck back to our condo. The doors were held open for us, and the bags were brought on the jet. I held Moet's hand as we boarded the jet. Champagne was served to us, with an array of different foods. We strapped in, and held hands, as we waited for take off. when the lights let us know we were able to walk around, we grabbed hands and went into the bedroom in the back.

"I've been wanting this pussy since last night," I whispered in her ear, as I lifted her shirt off and slid down her sweatpants.

"Hmm, come get this, baby," she moaned, as I pushed her back on the queen size bed. I wanted king, but this was the largest that would fit. She spread her legs open and patted her pussy.

I slid my pants down and threw my shirt off before pouncing on top of Moet. I kissed her lips, and slipped my fingers right into her warm cookies. She was fidgeting and moaning like I was giving her the dick. I slipped my fingers out and licked my fingers, and then slid right inside of her. I held her shoulders in place, as I slid deeper inside of her. She moved a little to allow all of me to fit inside.

"Yes, deeper babe," she moaned, as she scratched my back.

"Like that," I moaned back, going deeper, while I fondled her breasts.

She looked into my eyes, as I continued to make love to her. This wasn't fucking; I wasn't throwing her around, and having rough sex. We were taking our time, looking into each other's eyes, as I explored her insides. Her legs wrapped around my waist, as I placed kisses all over her neck and chest. I rolled over and pulled her on top of me. She slid down on my dick with ease, and slowly rode me. We looked into each other's eyes, as the sounds of wetness filled the room. I held her waist and gripped a piece of her ass, and she bent down and placed her lips on mine.

I sucked her tongue into my mouth, as our tongues did a little dance. I held onto her face and kissed her so hard. Damn, my feelings for this woman was deep and we hadn't been together that long. I never believed in love at first sight. You could see someone and fall in love with their appearance, and then they open their mouth and it all goes to hell. However, Moet was beautiful, intelligent and humble. Yeah, she was a little crazy, but who didn't need that?

"I love you, baby," I whispered, as I ran my hand through her hair.

She had her hair blown out, and I didn't understand why she wore a weave. "I love you too, Zyair," she said, sealing her statement with a kiss.

I felt her body tightening up, and she started moving her hips faster, so I flipped her over and shoved myself inside her warm opening. "Damn, you so tight," I moaned, as I slapped her ass.

She came all over my dick, as I looked at the bed getting wet with her juices. I pulled out, and came on her butt. She collapsed on the bed with her ass in the air, as I got a warm cloth from the bathroom to wipe her down.

"Come on, let's shower so we can have some breakfast," I picked her up and carried her to the bathroom.

*

I stood on the balcony as I watched the boats going back and forth on the canal. It was a little chilly, but nothing major. The sky was so blue, and reflected off the water. The hotel was right on the canal with all our windows facing the beautiful view. My girl was so different. Any other chick would have been excited to go to Bahamas, Aruba, or just anywhere tropical, but she wanted to come to Amsterdam. We hadn't been here for an hour and she already planned for us to see the Ann Frank Museum. She paid extra so we could skip the line. I was pissed because her ass paid for it, but I let her have that. When she was in the bathroom, I took her credit card and cash and placed it at the bottom of her suitcase.

"Baby, it's so beautiful here… I can't wait to get out there and see sights and take pictures. These are going in my scrapbook." She wrapped her arms around me.

"I'm more for smoking some weed, fucking and eating," I joked, and she mushed me in the back of my head.

"You've been to different countries, so you're used to this. Yet, I am not and we're going to sight see and do all the tourist things. We can fuck anytime at home, but we're going to be out and about." She popped her gums, and flipped her hair before walking back inside.

"Keep swinging that shit, I'm gonna pull it out." I mimicked like I was giving her back shots and pulling her hair.

"You so nasty; let's go," she yelled for me, and I put my jacket on and followed behind her.

We weren't due at the museum for a couple hours, so we got something to eat and walked around. We took a few pictures and silly videos before we settled on a bench. I sat on the top of the bench and she sat between my legs, and I caressed her shoulders. The people in the shop we stopped in told us *Vondel Park* was a tourist favorite and I could see why. The scenery was dope as fuck. On each tree, there were barriers that people used as lost and found. They clipped it to the gates on the tree. Shit, if that was New York, that shit would have been gone soon as a nigga dropped it. That just showed you how different places were. Everybody has a smile on their face, as they greeted us. It felt nice to be regular for once; no paparazzi, security and people screaming out to me. I knew it was only a matter of time before it happened, but I was enjoying the time while it lasted. Tulips were everywhere; I bent back and picked a few and handed it to Moet. She smiled and kissed me.

"I really appreciate you bringing me here, Zyair. A simple gift would have been fine, but you went above and beyond to put a smile on my face," she said, caressing the side of my face.

"You're not a simple girl, so nothing simple would do. I always want to keep that smile on your face. Even when you're being rolled over to get your Dependent changed."

She shoved me and laughed, snorting in the process. "You're so gross. Let's go feed the turtles and ducks."

My phone started ringing, and I had to take the call. "Babe, go ahead. Let me take this and then I'm coming."

She nodded, and went by the water to feed the ducks and turtles the left overs from her lox and bagel. I answered the phone and walked around so I could get better service. It was Hakeem calling me, so I knew it had to be important.

"What's good?"

"So, I cut my ties with Cabrina," he revealed.

I didn't give him an ultimatum, fire him or judge him. Money was money and he had to get it. Hearing this new shocked the hell out of me.

"What happened? I thought y'all was good?"

"She's demanding to be booked for some crazy shit that even I can't make happen. I'm good at what I do, but I can't make people accept her. Especially since she keeps making herself look crazy with you in the media. The cherry on the sundae was that she got picked for the new season of *Hollywood Exes*."

"She can't use me… Can she?"

"I don't know, but I'm going to have Navi call you lawyer and see what he can do. I know a similar thing happened with that football player, Micah Johnson. I mean, I could pull some strings and get his number so you can see what he did about it," he offered.

"Yeah, do that; I'm trying to make this a good birthday, so if I don't answer, go ahead and hit Navi up if you need anything."

"Fo' sure."

"You and Monett good?" I questioned.

"Yeah, we're straight. Ight, tell Moe I said happy birthday and y'all enjoy," he said, and we ended the call.

I walked back over to Moet who was in her own world. The happiness was evident on her face. She was in complete peace and I hated that was about to end. Cabrina going on this show was everything but good. I for sure knew Moet was going to flip her lid when she found out. I wrapped my arms around her and kissed her on the neck.

"Everything taken care of?"

"Yeah, some last minute things I didn't handle. You good?"

"I'm perfect; you ready to head to the museum?"

I grabbed her hand and nodded. "Let's go get some culture in," I smirked, and she shook her head. We headed to the museum, but my mind was on Cabrina's whack ass.

Chapter Four

Moet

The Anne Frank Museum was everything, and I enjoyed every part of it. I was obsessed with anything that had to do with either Anne Frank or World War II. Zane was interested too, because he kept asking questions because he couldn't believe some of the history. It was definitely worth the three hours we spent inside of there. After seeing all of that, we decided to go to a coffee shop called *Dampkring.* We got a table and the waitress got us some coffee and a menu. For some reason, it still surprised me that they had weed on the menu. I ordered some coffee and we both agreed to order some weed. We settled on the Kandy Kush and some Hashish.

"There's a way that we do it here in Amsterdam," the woman said with an accent. It wasn't as deep, but she spoke good English.

"Oh yeah? What's that?"

"Let me go get your things and I'll be right back," she insisted, so we sat and sipped our coffee and ate the treats they had available.

"These weed brownies are fuckin' good," Zane said, damn near yelling.

The lady came back with ashtrays, papers, and of course the weed. She rolled the first one mixing the Hashish and the Kandy Kush together. She lit it and handed it to me. I took a pull and choked, and handed it to Zane.

"Shit… This some good shit," he blew out smoke rings.

"Enjoy," she smiled, and left to serve other tables.

We passed the blunts back and forth, as I checked my messages. When I finished, the plate of weed brownies was gone, and Zane was doing the bounce with his shoulders. "This music is bumping," he said, with his eyes the color of Satan.

"You high as fuck," I laughed, as I took the weed and took a pull. "This shit is fucking strong as hell," I giggled.

"I milly rock on all these blocks…" He got up and started dancing.

He was high as fuck and I couldn't stop laughing. I knew I was high as fuck too, but this nigga was wilding. I knew it was from those damn brownies. I had weed brownies one time in college, and that taught my ass to stay away from them shits. They got you higher than smoking.

"Babe, those aren't even the words," I laughed, with tears coming down my eyes.

He sat down and looked to the side of us. The look on his face was terrified, as he moved back fast as hell. "Moet, you don't see those fucking bunnies running around? Come on, this shit is nasty. Bunnies running around a bar," he vented, and snatched his jacket off the back of his chair.

I paid the tab with his credit card and ran to catch up with him. I was high, but once the air hit me, I felt a little better. But this nigga was jumping and saying he saw all kind of crazy shit. "Let's catch a cab and go to the hotel," I offered, rubbing his back.

He was really scared, and I guess he must have been really seeing the shit he was calling out. "Babe, I don't feel right for real," he said, pulling my hair, so I looked him in his wide ass eyes.

I tried my best to stifle the laugh, but I couldn't help it and burst out laughing in his face; this shit was too hilarious. We got a cab and headed back to the hotel. The whole ride he was yelling about shit he was 'seeing'. This birthday had to be the best birthday I had ever had. I was with my baby, he was high and I was in a different country. This felt right on all levels.

"We're here, babe," I said nudging him. That fast his ass had fallen asleep. He said inaudible words, but he was carrying himself inside the hotel. Thankfully, I didn't have to damn near carry him inside.

When we got into the hotel, he went straight to the bed and laid down with his clothes on. I took his boots off and jacket, and covered him up. I grabbed my cell phone and dialed Tammy. She called me earlier, but we were at the museum and phones weren't allowed. My ass was going to pay for this shit later with roaming charges.

"Happy birthday, baby!" she squealed into the phone.

"Thank you, cupcake! What are you doing?"

"I'm at my doctor's appointment now, and then me and Rick are having a lunch date," she explained, sounding in good spirits.

"Damn, it's dinner time here… Zyair's crazy ass brought me to Amsterdam," I revealed, and she laughed.

"I knew all about that. He told me when he paid for the hotel. Are you having a good time?"

"We smoked some weed and Zy ate some weed brownies and his ass was bugging the fuck out," I giggled.

She started laughing so hard that she was choking in the background. "Damn, you should have recorded that shit."

"You think I didn't? I sent it all to my emails in case he tried to delete while I'm sleep. That shit was hilarious," I laughed again.

"I'm happy you are enjoying yourself."

"I am; so what happened at your appointment?"

"They retrieved the eggs and shit. I'm a little sore, so Rick's mother has Dion again. I swear once this is over, I am taking my baby and husband and we're gonna be locked in the house. I feel like I never get to spend time with her anymore. She's growing up quick, Moe," she sighed.

"I know; time waits for no one. You and Rick need some time alone too, so y'all can relax and be with each other… You know?"

"Yeah, I know. Call me later and we'll talk. Have fun, baby," she yelled, as I laughed at her ratchet ass.

"Later, boo." I ended the call and got into bed with Zane. I was tired as hell too, and tomorrow I had a full day planned for us."

*

I heard metal clicking and clacking as I tried to get my last little bit of sleep for the morning. Yet, Zane wasn't letting that happen this morning. He got into the bed with a tray of breakfast and nudged me, with his mouth filled.

"Babe, come get some food. I'm starving like a muthafucka and might finish this," he smacked into my ears.

I opened my eyes one by one, as I pulled myself up and rested my back on the headboard. I looked over at him and he was pouring syrup on his eggs, which turned me off to the whole breakfast.

"I'll take some bacon and toast. You can have the rest," I yawned and went to brush my teeth. As I was passing the window, I noticed that it was raining – hard. This ruined my plans since all the things I had planned were outdoors.

"I was thinking we'll stay an extra day to make up for this rain day," he offered once I came out the bathroom.

"That doesn't sound too bad, but it's cool. We don't have to."

I sat on the bed and ate the bacon and toast, as I scrolled down Monett's Instagram. My face lit up whenever I saw my nephew. I was having serious baby fever, and it seemed like everywhere I turned, it was some more things involving babies. I liked the picture and commented on a few. I watched Zane watching me out the side of my eye, as I looked at a picture of Nauti a little too long.

"Be honest with me," he smacked, as he put more syrup on his eggs.

I closed my phone and looked at him. "Of course; what's up?"

"You want a baby, don't you?" He looked at me seriously, and I looked away. His stare was too intense.

Looking down at my coffee, I decided to answer him. "I… I mean I do, but I know it'll happen in a couple years. I don't want to push you into something you're not ready for," I stuttered a little.

I had all the time in the world to have children, and I was going to be married and should enjoy my newlywed years with my husband first. However, I wanted a child and seeing Monett with Nauti, and Tammy trying to have another made me want one. I mean, it could be a phase, but for the past couple of weeks, all that had been on mind was babies, marriage and work.

"Moet, you can't dictate how I feel about something without asking me. If I'm not ready, I'll let you know, but you won't know unless you ask… feel me?"

I nodded my head. "I hear you."

"If you want a baby, fuck it, let's make one," he nonchalantly said, and I screwed my face up.

"If *I* want a baby? Zyair, this isn't a pet, this is a child. A piece of me and you, not some yorkie we're getting from the pet shop… Just forget about it." I waved him off and went into the kitchen.

I went into the fridge and poured me some orange juice, and he closed the door before I could get the container out. "You don't think I want this? I wouldn't be talking about making one if I didn't want one, Moe," his voice softened and he touched my face.

"Just forget that we even talked about this," I insisted, and tried to walk out the kitchen, but he blocked me.

"I'm not going to forget about it it because this is something you want. Bae, why are we fighting about this?" he asked, running his hands through my hair.

I sighed and leaned back on the counter. "I don't know. I want a baby, but then I don't want to look like we're just rushing into things without thinking about it. You know Tammy and Rick are trying for another baby?" I looked up into his eyes.

"I heard something about that. She was telling me about it the other day. Is this what that's about? Monett and Tammy? You feel like you need to have one now?"

"No… I mean, I don't know, but I know when I hold my nephew or see a baby while I'm working, I just feel like I could do that," I tried to explain my feelings.

"Do what?"

"Be a mother. Love a child and be everything to the one person that could hear my heart beat from the inside," I said taking a quote I saw on Facebook, but it was true. That's how I was feeling.

"Peanut, you know the situation with my moms and with my pops. Besides Tammy and Big Mama, that's all I got. So, if you're ready to have a baby, I'm ready too." He hugged me, and I sighed. "Now what?"

"I don't know, just a lot to think about it."

He picked me up and I giggled. "How about we go have unprotected sex, and I release my kids in your park and if it happens, it happens."

I laughed at his example of making a baby and kissed him. "Deal."

He lifted me higher and bit my ass, as I giggled. "Let's start right now." He bit my ass again, while I laughed and he carried me to the room.

I don't know if I was ready for a baby, but I wanted one. Time would only tell if I was ready for a child, when I was blessed with one. However, trying and having fun doing it wouldn't be wrong… right?

Monett

"I'm about sick of your attitude when I come home from work," John slurred, as he walked through the door towards me.

I walked back into the kitchen and continued to wash the dishes. My back was killing me and I felt like I couldn't breathe all day. I spent the day resting and catching up on some shows I may have missed during the week. I also managed to cook dinner for Johnathan, and waited two hours for him to come in from work.

"All I ask is for you to come home and spend time with me. Is that too much to ask?" I questioned, while I held a plate in one hand and a dishrag in the other.

"Bitch, I make the money and deserve to go out and have a couple drinks!" he continued to yell.

We lived in a townhouse, so the houses were all connected. A couple times, our neighbors didn't hesitate to call the police about our arguments. Often, I'd have to tell them that I was fine and my neighbors were overreacting, while covering up a fresh bruise. Johnathan swung his body onto the couch and kicked his filthy work boots up on the coffee table. He snatched the remote off the other side of the couch and flipped through the channels.

"John, we have a baby coming; a baby that you wanted so badly that you..." I couldn't even bring myself to say the words.

"So badly that what?" He abandoned the couch and walked toward me. I could tell he was drunk, if his slurring and actions wasn't enough to warn me.

"Nothing," I replied, and walked back to the sink.

"No, I want to hear it come out your mouth," he snickered, and grabbed a hand full of my hair. He yanked my head back and looked into my eyes. "Come on, speak," he encouraged, pulling my head back a little more.

Tears spilled out my eyelids, as I tried to free myself. I wish I could say that he was only abusive when he was drunk; however, that wasn't the case. If things weren't his way, he'd be abusive. Something in his mother's eyes told me to run, but I was so hell bent in love with him.

"That you forced me to have sex without protection," I winced when he pulled my hair back.

"You damn right... That pussy is mine, and you're going to be my wife and children's mother, you hear?" he spoke directly in my ear. His spit hitting the inside of my ears, as the smell of alcohol invaded my nostrils.

"Yes," I mumbled. I felt his hand loosen and then felt him slam my head onto the countertop as he...

"Stoppppppp pleaseee, pleaseeeee!" I screamed, while fighting for him to get off of me.

"Monett, Monett," I heard someone calling me, but I was still fighting. I felt a pair of hands gently wrap around me, and I opened my eyes and saw Hakeem.

My heart was beating out my chest, as the sweat poured down my face. In fact, the whole side of my bed was wet with sweat. I sat up and looked around the room before jumping up, but Hakeem grabbed me gently.

"Calm down, baby… you're good," he whispered, as he pulled me into his hard chest.

"I… I gotta go check on Nauti," I whimpered, but he didn't let me go. I was visibly shaken up and hadn't had a nightmare like this in a while.

"Babe, he's good right now. You going in there like that is going to wake him up. What were you dreaming about?" He rubbed my hair, as he picked me up and carried me to the bathroom.

He sat me down on the bench, undressed me and ran the shower. I was still breathing hard, and waiting for this nice treatment to end. He lifted me up and put me in the shower, where he stood fully clothed. He washed my hair and body, as he kissed me and told me I was going to be alright.

"It…It was Johnathan," I whispered, and he stopped washing me up and looked at me.

He lifted my face up and looked me in the eyes. He noticed how sad and scared I was from the nightmare I just had. "Why you wait so long to tell me, Monett?"

"I just…I just…" I broke down and started crying. I fell to the floor, and Hakeem got down with me and pulled me into his arms.

"You just what? You need to speak to me, Monett!" He shook me, and all I could do was cry.

Sensing that I wouldn't be any good to answer questions right now, he finished washing me up and put me in some pajamas. I laid in the bed, while looking up at the ceiling with a million thoughts clouding my head. Johnathan hurt me badly, so bad that I had emotional wounds I was still dealing with. But, I still wanted to protect him and make sure that no harm came his way. Why did I feel like that? It made me so angry that I thought like that, but I couldn't change it. My heart wouldn't allow me to hurt him the same way he hurt me. Eventually, my eyes got heavy and I fell back to sleep. Hakeem went into his office after he got me dressed; I guess he was upset.

The sun shined right on my face and I threw the blanket over my face to shield it. I peeked out and looked at the time, before I closed the blinds with the remote and got out of bed. Hakeem wasn't in bed, and Nauti wasn't in his crib when I looked at the baby monitor. I walked out the room and Nauti was sitting in his bouncer on the counter, while Hakeem made breakfast. I sat at the stool and looked at him.

"You ready to talk yet?" he softly asked. I expected him to be upset and tune me out, but he looked genuinely concerned.

"Yes," I responded, accepting the plate of food he pushed in front of me.

"I'm listening."

"John was the one who pushed me off the road. He was drunk and came to my appointment acting a fool and then… it happened," I vaguely explained. I didn't feel like getting into it about what happened.

"Why didn't you inform the police?"

"I don't want things coming back to him, Hakeem. He was rotten to me, but he had a fucked up upbringing. I just want to do the right thing and not be crucified for it."

"Monett, that isn't the right thing to do. You're making excuses for a grown ass man that had a choice… You think…" He started, but then stopped.

"You think what?" I pushed, accepting the orange juice.

"Nothing," he dryly replied, as he busied himself with cleaning his mess up in the kitchen.

"How do you expect me to be honest with you when you're hiding shit?" I voiced, and he turned and faced me.

My eyes softened as I looked at this man. I didn't want to hide things from him, or build our relationship on lies. My last relationship was built on so much that the lies was the least thing. I wanted to know everything about my partner, and vice versa.

"Look, I never had it easy growing up and I didn't make excuses. I could have been a drug dealer or whatever, and used my environment as an excuse, but I didn't. I made shit happen to get where I am today," he disclosed.

"I understand-"

"Nah, you don't understand. You didn't get raised in a trap house, your crib being raided damn near every week, or waking up to go piss and seeing your pops smoking weed, while watching your moms get raw dogged by three niggas at the same time. I could have easily stepped into the life, but I didn't. When I graduated high school, I went to college and then moved to Hollywood and waited for my chance. I managed to become a manager for a few upcoming rappers, but got my break when I met Cabrina." He placed the glasses into the cabinet. "She moved here from Virginia and needed and wanted a chance. We built a genuine friendship, but once she started booking gigs, she changed. I managed a couple of other people before I got my chance to manage Zane. I have other clients too, but Zane is my biggest yet."

"Damn baby, I didn't know all of that," I said, amazed at his story. He vaguely told me things, but I never pushed. I felt if someone wanted to tell to tell you something, they would.

"Shit wasn't easy. There was a lot of shit that happened that made me want to give up and get it the fast way, but I didn't."

I abandoned the counter, and walked over to him and wrapped my arms around him. I laid my head on his chest and looked up at him. "I'm proud of you baby… Can I ask you a question?"

"What's that?" he rubbed my back and kissed my forehead.

"Do you still have a relationship with your parents?"

"I send money to my mother and visit her whenever I'm in California, but we don't have a relationship. As for my pops, he's serving a life sentence for murder."

I shook my head and held his face, and kissed him. "My family is your family now," I smiled, and placed a kiss on his lips.

"Yeah, that's all nice, but what we gonna do about this shit you just told me?" He waved off my little touching moment, but I kind of knew that would happen.

"Nothing, we're going to do nothing. Just let it be, Hakeem." I went to go pick up Nauti.

"How do you expect me to just do nothing about what you told me? He could have killed both you and Nauti," he expressed, and I rolled my eyes wishing that I didn't share that information.

"He didn't; let's drop it and handle it when he comes out of rehab," I slipped and said.

"Now the nigga is doing drugs… Damn Monett," he sighed, and went into his office.

The apartment was slowly coming together, but Hakeem's office was still in the process of getting put together. He sat behind his desk and got on his computer. I sat down in one of the plush chairs and cuddled Nauti.

"He has a problem with alcohol. After the accident, he visited me and explained that he needs to get help and he's sorry. You can look at me however you want, but I believe in second chances, and I don't want to take him away from his son unless he gives me another reason."

"Second chances my ass. Moet know about this?"

"No, and she won't, right?" I looked at him sternly, and he shook his head.

"Monett, don't expect me to be all welcoming. You're going to do what you want anyway, so it's whatever. I know that nigga better not bring his ass in my crib."

"Ours."

"Huh?"

"Our crib," I corrected him.

"Mine, yours, ours, his ass better not bring his ass up in here. And you better do visitation visit with his ass. Continue to keep your issues to yourself, if you're not going to solve them." He got up and went into the bedroom. I shook my head and went to go handle Nauti's demands for the day.

Tammy

It had been a couple weeks since my last doctor's appointment and here I was staring at the positive pregnancy test in my hand. I didn't know how to feel about the situation. I was excited to be with child again, yet, my mind was on Rick. Lately, he hadn't been in the best health. He was sick most of the time and didn't have energy to even smoke to get an appetite. His doctor sent a nurse to the house to place a tube in his stomach that would give him nutrition. No matter how hard or bad he felt, he still kept a smile on his face and joked around. I slid down onto the floor in the bathroom and looked at the pregnancy test. Why did this have to be my life? Why couldn't my husband be happy and healthy? I knew not to question God, but I couldn't help but not question the choices He was making for my life. My house phone rang and I looked at the caller ID before answering the phone; it was Big Mama.

"Hey Big Mama," I dryly greeted.

"What's the matter, Tamala?" she questioned.

I didn't speak to Big Mama much because she always made me cry, and think about shit I tend to push out of mind. Plus, she ran her mouth to my mother too much, which I hated. "Just overwhelmed about everything. I'll be fine… You coming to New York for Thanksgiving?"

"Zyair is flying me in for the holidays. I'll be in New York until after the New Year," she told me and I smiled.

"At least I'll have some time with you before you go."

"Uh huh, I spoke to your mother; what's going on with that?"

"I ran into her a couple weeks ago, but nothing has happened since then. I don't need or want her in my life," I replied, rolling my eyes. I was so done with my mother and didn't need her in my life.

"Tamala, you need to forgive your mother. You only get on mother, so you need to pull together and make this work with her."

Knock! Knock!

I cracked the door open and it was Rick's doctor. "I wanna speak to you before I leave," she told me, and I nodded, while holding the phone piece away from me. After Rick refused treatment, Zyair stopped paying and receiving advice from that doctor. At first he agreed with the doctor about Rick stopping treatment, but then when he went home, he felt like the doctor didn't fight hard enough for his patient. So, he found the best oncologist in the country. She lived in Alaska, but he flew her and her team into New York to personally go over Rick's case. I loved my cousin because he went above and beyond and didn't think twice.

"Big Mama, I gotta go. Rick's doctor wants to speak to me. I'll call you later… Better yet, I'll see you in a couple days," I laughed.

"Alright, love you, Tammy."

"Love you too, Big Mama."

I picked myself up off the floor and fixed myself, before putting the pregnancy test in the medicine cabinet. I washed my hands and left the bathroom. I found her sitting in the living room, tapping in information on her medical tablet.

"How are you, Mrs. Smith?" She greeted, and shook my hand.

"I'm doing fine, considering." I returned her hand shake, and sat down and crossed my legs.

She started shifting through different papers and looked up at me. Right about now I didn't have any patience, and the more she shifted those papers, the more I was ready to go off.

"Alright, so as you know I've been reviewing your husband's medical information for a little over a month. Your cousin, Mr. Whitfield, requested my knowledge to explore every option that we have for your husband. Me and my colleague have been looking over his scans that his previous doctor sent over and we're actually astonished." She set her tablet down and leaned forward.

"Astonished about?"

"People come to my offices in Alaska just to get a second opinion because my work with cancer has been so remarkable… Not tooting my own horn, but I am the best. Now, I don't like to talk about other doctors, but when I have a patient like your husband who was clearly given a death sentence, I try and find every roadway to deter that cancer and prolong that death sentence. Your husband's previous doctors, and the doctors Mr. Whitfield hired before me are complete idiots, excuse my language." I went to the corner of our living room and offered her some sparkling water from the bar. She accepted the drink, moistened her mouth and cleared her throat.

"Wait… I'm so confused… What are you saying?"

"I'm saying you should get you a lawyer, sweetheart," she nodded her head.

"A lawyer? For what?"

She picked back up the papers and huge envelopes she had, and pulled something else out of the envelope. They were X-rays. She flipped through some papers and laid them out on the coffee table before me. Holding up the first X-ray, she pointed to a specific spot. "I went over your husband's charts since he was a teenager, getting antibiotics for a little STD he had back in tenth grade. I basically feel like I know his body in and out, and looking at these scans, your husband doesn't have stage four bone cancer."

My first shock was Rick having a damn STD; we were dating then, and I damn sure ain't have no sexually transmitted disease, and then it dawned on me what she just said. "So, what does he have?"

"At most, I would say he has stage two cancer. Those tumors on his bones aren't anything near stages three to four," she said, and pulled out another X-Ray and showed me the difference. "You see, Rick and this patient's scans are nothing to compare, because it's evident."

"So, why did he get worst? He was fine when he stopped treatment and medicine, and now he has a stomach tube and too sick to eat."

I wasn't going to get my hopes up just to be crushed again. I was finally coming to the terms that my husband was going to die. I wasn't going to let this pale bitch fill my head with false hope, just to snatch it away when her ass rode her polar bear back to Alaska.

"Mrs. Smith, I didn't say the cancer is gone; I said he has stage two. He's still going to get sick, but the range of treatment your husband's previous doctors and the doctors Mr. Whitfield hired used, were aggressive forms of chemo that would make anyone as weak as your husband became. I'm assuming they didn't do the amount of research we did, and just went based off the information that was sent over from your husband's doctors. I'm no lawyer, but I believe you have a malpractice suit."

I had to uncross my legs and lean up and really listen to this woman. "Who would I sue? You're saying they all basically misdiagnosed him."

"Both of them, Mrs. Smith. Your husband went through aggressive rounds of chemo for months, was given treatments that weren't for his diagnosis, and not to mention the emotional toll it put on your family. I'm not telling you what to do, but I would look into filing a law suit, and doing it quickly. As for your husband, we have implemented a plan of treatment that we'll be starting. He's agreed, signed off on it and is ready to receive it," she informed me.

"Rick signed off on it?" I asked shocked as hell. He was adamant about not going through any treatment.

"Of course, it took a little convincing on my part, but he's agreed to do it."

"What's the treatment?"

She handed me a bunch of brochures, papers and medical research that she had. Some papers had her handwriting scribbled all over it. "We're going to start with Hormone therapy. Rick will receive bisphosphonates by IV infusion every three to four weeks. The drugs help with bone metastasis, by slowing bone damage and reducing the risk of bone fractures, easing bone pain and reducing high levels of calcium in the blood," she explained. It was clear that she took her job serious.

"Okay, I'm liking this… So this will be able to help with his walking and stuff?"

"Absolutely; now there are some side effects, and they are listed in those papers. However, I haven't had a patient with side effects yet. Now, we're also going to do immunotherapy. This helps his immune system spot and more effectively kills cancer cells. Some methods of immunotherapy have been used for a while, and some are still experimental."

"So, let me get this straight. Rick agreed to all of this?"

"Yes, he did. He knows it's going to be a little tough, but if he can beat this, it'll be amazing."

I had tears streaming down my eyes as I thought of the fact that my husband might have a standing chance to kick cancer's ass. "He'll still continue with chemo, but not as aggressive as what he's been getting. You're almost at the end of the tunnel," she winked, and started gathering her things.

"Thank you so much, Dr. Hanna," I hugged her, and I usually didn't hug folks. I felt like she was the closet thing to God right now.

"You're welcome. He has an appointment this week. I'll have my assistant to call you to confirm. Also, stop letting him smoke marijuana," she winked, and left out the door.

I danced all the way to Rick's room, where he was watching TV. "So, you heard the good news?" he smirked, and I climbed into the bed with him.

"I guess I'll keep you around a little longer," I kissed his lips, as he gripped my ass.

I mushed his head and he looked at me confused. "Who you got a STD from in the tenth grade?"

He chuckled and covered my mouth with his. I was going to keep the pregnancy a secret, but I couldn't wait to tell Moet about the news. I couldn't keep shit from her nosy ass anyway.

Zane

"You dead ass? Yo Tammy, that shit is awesome, and I think we need to get my legal team together and handle this," I advised, and I heard her suck her teeth.

"Zyair, it isn't about the money, honestly. I'm just happy my husband has a small window of hope; you know?"

"I feel you, Tam. Yet, these doctors almost killed your husband and caused so much grief over this. You need to pursue this so it doesn't happen to anyone else. We know you don't need the money, but it's the principle. You can settle for all I care, but let them know that you know about this, and you're taking action."

"I guess so," she hesitantly replied.

"Cool, I'll get my legal team to draw up everything. All you have to do is provide Rick's papers and show up in court. You know me and Moe will be there," I assured her.

"I'm a grown ass woman, I don't need y'all," she joked and I laughed, because her ghetto ass was back.

"Yeah, whatever… I'll call you later. Oh, and Big Mama's staying with you," I slid that in there, and she choked on whatever she was smacking on in my ear.

"With me?" she choked out.

"She insisted," I continued to fuck with her. Moet already had one of the guest rooms prepped for Big Mama's arrival.

"You know what, Zy-"

"I'm fucking with you, Tam. But, you need to spend some time with her while she's here."

"Yeah, yeah. My baby is up from her nap, so I'll call your Kevin Hart ass back," she snickered and ended the call.

I laughed and shook my head, as I hung up the phone and continued to eat breakfast. I had to be at the gym in a couple hours. Since I got back to New York, I had been slacking and haven't been going to the gym and training. When Hakeem called me about a fight that was taking place in Miami in a couple weeks, my ass got back in the gym quick. It had been a couple weeks since we got back from Amsterdam. When we both agreed to have a baby, I didn't think Moet was going to take this shit so serious. We fucked damn near everyday, and when she couldn't find me at home, she came to the gym and fucked me in the locker room. Now, I was down for sex all the time, especially with Moet. Yet, she was taking this baby shit too far and it was making sex a job between us.

I mean, when I told her we could have a baby, I honestly thought it was a phase she was going through. She always told me she wasn't ready for children and she had her God daughter. I was witnessing a different Moet and that shit was slowly making me reconsider what I said. I finished my oatmeal and went into the bedroom. She wasn't in bed anymore, so I went into the bathroom. I heard sniffling coming from the water closet, and opened it. Moet was sitting on the floor with a pregnancy test and tears streaming down her face.

"Peanut, what's good with you?" I said, pulling her up and wrapping my arms around her.

She handed me the negative pregnancy test and broke down and continued to cry. "We've fucked a million times, and when I was ovulating… Why is it still negative?"

See what I mean? She was like a different Moet when it came to this baby making shit. "Ma, this shit isn't going to happen over night. Be patient and stop stressing yourself about this. Look at you crying over this." I kissed her on the lips, and she bypassed me and went to the sink.

"I missed my period, Zane. I thought I was pregnant and then I take a test and it's negative. What am I missing?" she slapped her thighs and went into the closet. She pulled her scrubs, sneakers and things out for the day.

"You're thinking too much into this shit, Moet."

She scoffed at me, and turned on the shower. "I'm glad to see that this is just considered shit to you. Why did you agree in Amsterdam if this doesn't mean shit to you!" she yelled and undressed.

"When did you start stressing over wanting a baby, Moet? Last we spoke you said you weren't ready for children. Is it because of Monett?"

She looked at me through the glass shower door, and rolled her eyes. "I've always wanted a baby, Zane. I wanted one with Ki, but he couldn't get his shit together. He promised, and promised, and promised he would get himself together so we could have a baby. Imagine my surprise when Monett announces that she's pregnant. So, of course I had to act like I didn't want children."

"So now seeing her with your nephew brought that shit back?"

She rinsed off and stepped out the shower with a huge cotton towel wrapped around her. "Refer to this situation as shit again, I dare you," she threatened, and went into our bedroom.

I followed behind her and sat on the edge of the bed, while watching her lotion her body. Damn, her body looked so good. "My bad, Peanut. Let me pick you up tonight and we'll go have some dinner and spend some time. We've both been working and need some time. I'm not trying to feel like I'm married before we're actually married," I laughed, and she looked at me with tight lips.

"Sounds good with me, baby." She walked over to me and kissed me on the lips, before slipping her shoes on and putting her scrub top on. "See you later." She continued gathering her things and left me sitting there, stuck. Man, women were some strange creatures.

Since I was dressed, I headed out not too long after her. I was going over Hakeem's crib to talk about some business, but I could get his advice on this shit too. He was always the calm in my storm. I took my Porsche and burnt rubber down the New York City streets, until I arrived at Hakeem and Monett's condo. I had the valet take my whip, and hopped out. I was let upstairs and knocked on their door. Monett answered, looking beautiful. I had never saw her before she was pregnant, but I'm guessing that's what Hakeem must have envisioned when he locked her down. She didn't even look like she had a baby a couple weeks ago, which was amazing to me. From her physique, she was thick, but a little leaner than Moet.

"Damn, where did you put the baby weight, Monett?" I joked, as she hugged me.

"Zane, knock it off; you don't see these hips and thighs? Hakeem is in his office; you need anything?" She walked around the kitchen counter, where her little man was sitting.

I usually wasn't interested in babies, but I decided to go and look at his growth, since I hadn't been able to come see him. I looked at him and smiled. It was no doubt this baby was mixed; however, he looked just like his mother.

"Damn, he looks just like you," I complimented and she smiled.

"I hear that all the damn time, and he acts just like his spoiled ass aunt. How is she this morning? I called to see if me and Nauti could come take her out to lunch, and she went off and hung up on me. Y'all having problems?" she narrowed her eyes at me and I laughed.

I was smart enough not to repeat all that Moet told me this morning. If she didn't tell her sister, it wasn't my business to tell. "We're all good, she probably got her lady shit."

"Her period?" Monett clarified.

"Yeah… That." I hightailed it to Hakeem's office down the hall. I wasn't getting caught up in whatever she and Moet was going through. Shit, she went off on my ass this morning too, but I wasn't going to openly admit that.

Knock! Knock!

I walked into the room and Hakeem was on the phone. He motioned for me to close the door and sit down. I sat down and looked around his office; it was cool. He had a bunch of pictures and knick knacks around. He finished his call and hung up the phone before turning his attention back to me.

"What's good, nigga?" He dapped hands with me, and sat back down.

"I came to talk some business with you, bruh. You tell me about this fight but don't give me no details."

"That's because I'm still nailing those down, but this is going to happen so I need you in the gym."

"I'm on my way there soon as I leave from here. Where is it going to be held?" I watched as he went into the mini fridge and threw me a bottle of water.

"The details are still being etched out. You know it takes time to get everything in whole, but right now I told them our price, and they're working it out. I also got some information about the Cabrina situation. I pulled some strings and spoke to Micah Johnson and he was amused by your situation. He said it wasn't anything he could really do, but he did have the production company blur his name and bleep out his name."

"Bullshit," I sighed, thinking about how this shit would bother Moet.

"Just talk to her before the season starts filming. It'll be all over once it starts, so talk to her about it."

"Yeah, I'm gonna do that tonight. Hopefully she don't kill my ass."

"Trouble in paradise?" He leaned up and took a piece of candy out the bowl.

"When we were in Amsterdam, she brought up babies."

"She wants a baby? Since when?"

"Man, she's always wanted a baby. But now she wants one and I told her we can make one, but I created a monster. We fuck all the time and she's stressing out and shit. I found her in the bathroom crying this morning because she wasn't pregnant."

"That six weeks is creeping up on Monett, so if y'all wanna take Nauti to fulfill y'all baby fever, be my guest," he joked and I laughed.

"Nah, I'm good. I'm gonna talk to her about it tonight."

"That's the best you can do. It'll happen."

"Yeah, I know. Let me get out of here and to the gym. Hit me about that fight and let me know if it's a done deal." We dapped hands and I headed to the Gym. I had Navi make arrangements for dinner tonight."

Chapter Five

Moet

Y'all are probably reading this and thinking I'm tripping and to be honest, I am. You ever get with a guy and you're dating and things are going great. Then, you're laying in bed and look up at them while all their attention is on the TV, and you're thinking they'll make an amazing father or husband? Well, I had that moment the minute I met Zyair Zane Whitfield. I could picture him being my other half and raising our children together, with the dog and white picket fence. I once felt this way about Ki. Now, I know I was tripping and he wasn't meant to own a dog, more or less raise a child. I remember crying to Tammy about wanting to have his child, and even contemplated getting pregnant and raising my child alone.

With Zane things were different, and I wanted to be his wife and mother of his child. Shit, I was tired of being single and lonely Moet who worked all the time. I wanted to come home to a family of my own.

"Moet, take patient in room 312," a nurse said, slapping the file chart in front of me. I should have stayed my ass home because I was working in the ER tonight, and this was the last place I wanted or needed to be.

I rolled my eyes, dragged the file along the desk and walked to the room. I had an hour until I was off of work and instead of letting me fade to the background so I could clock out, they wanted to force me to see other patients. I opened the chart as I neared the door, looked through charts and walked through the door. When I looked at the name and looked up, I wanted to walk out the room.

"Blakeisha? That's so ghetto," I said, forgetting I was supposed to be professional. As much as I hated this bitch, I loved my career ten times more. I adjusted my attitude and continued looking through her chart. "I apologize," I mumbled.

"What brings you in, Ms. Brix?"

"Damn, I keep explaining this over and over. I'm four months pregnant and I'm spotting and I have a lot of pain," she explained, and I couldn't help the eye roll that occurred.

"Let me take your vital signs. When did this spotting start?" I continued to question, as I wrapped the blood pressure cuff around her arm.

"Last night; I tried to ignore it but it got worst, and when I woke up it was a little darker."

"Hmm... okay, your vital signs are good. The doctor will be in with you shortly."

"Umm, can you call the baby's father?"

Although my back was turned, I was pretty sure that she saw the major screw face I had on. I adjusted my face and looked at my beautiful engagement ring. "Sure, write down his number and I'll give him a call for you," I replied, trying to be sweet.

"Moet, can you finish your notes and don't forget to write the ones for the patient too," my supervisor reminded me.

"Got it." I walked back over to the computer next to her bed. I barely wanted to be near her to check her vitals. Now, I had to be sitting next to her while I typed in all this information. I usually just wrote it on a paper and left it for a newer nurse to fill in. "Give me a second to go over this stuff again with you," I sighed.

"Spotting, cramps... right?"

"Yes."

"Are you vomiting, nauseous or anythi-"

Ring! Ring!

"Give me a second," I said, and answered my phone and continued filling in information I did know. "Hey, what happened?" I answered.

"I'm done at the gym. I'm 'bout to head home and change, and I'll be heading to pick you up for tonight."

"Sounds like a plan, baby. Where we going?"

"Dinner, but don't worry about all that. You want me to bring you some clothes?"

"Umm, yeah, look in my closet on the rack near my jewelry island, there is a white Givenchy sweater, leggings and a pair of Valentino booties that Navi had the stylist lay out for me. Grab the matching clutch and some hoop earrings, and a long chunky necklace and I'm good."

"Damn, Givenchy… The stylist stays hooking you up," he faked gripped.

"You the one that wanted me to have a stylist so don't complain. I'm fine with my clo-"

"Yeah, yeah, yeah; it's a crime to spoil my girl. I'll grab all your girly shit, so be ready."

"Okay."

"Love you, Peanut."

"Love you too, Zyair," I cooed and hung the phone up.

"Y'all doing it like that now?" I jumped, because I forgot this bitch was still in the damn room. Whenever I spoke with Zyair, it was like I was in a different world.

"Excuse me?" I continued doing the notes. Since she was going to be my last patient, I decided to do all my charts so I could leave as soon as it was my time.

"I mean, y'all haven't been together a full year and you're already in his house with a closet and his stylist?"

"Well damn, you aren't discreet about your nosiness," I snapped, and she shrugged her shoulders like she was proud.

"You all in here giggling and supposed to be my nurse," she smiled, and I let my attitude down. I guess I shouldn't still be so nasty since I came off winning. "Damn, that ring is pretty."

"Thank you. Yes, we live together because we're about to be married, so it's not a problem to live together and share things."

"You right."

"The doctor will be in soon, but I need some urine in this cup and I need to take some blood, so I'll be back."

I walked out the room and ran straight into the doctor. "Moet, I'm sorry; is the patient ready?"

"Yep, just getting some urine and blood now, but that can wait," I said, purposely wanting to prolong that.

"Let me examine her and I'll request the results when I'm done."

"Okay, I'll call her child's father like she requested."

"Perfect."

I handed off the lab tray to another nurse and went to go make the call. I stopped and got me some chips and a soda, because I had about fifteen minutes and I planned to sit and eat these chips, while waiting for the clock to do its thing. I sat down and Zyair texted me to let me know he was outside. I grabbed the phone and dialed the number she gave me.

"Hello, I am calling on behalf of Blakeisha Brix. She's in the emergency room at Brooklyn Hospital," I started.

"Who the hell is that?" I recognized his voice immediately.

"Blake; she's in the emergency room with cramps and she's pregnant. She wants you to come."

"Moet?"

"Thank you, sir, she'll see you when you arrive." I hung up the phone and damn near ran to the office and clocked out. I grabbed my stuff and walked past Blake's room where she was hysterically crying. I was going to be sure to ask tomorrow once I clocked in.

When I walked out the hospital, Zyair was standing there with a dozen roses and a smile. I jumped into my baby's arms and kissed him. I wasn't thinking about earlier and my little meltdown. I was focused on my boo, and giving him my love and attention.

"Thank you, baby," I cooed, kissing him on his juicy lips.

"You welcome, ma. Go change so we can get our night started," he smirked, and gently slapped my ass.

"Oh, you gonna keep me out all night?" I flirted, and he nodded his head.

"I'm gonna keep you out and up all night," he shot back, and I hurried my ass into the hospital to quickly change.

After I changed, I met him back outside, and that's when I noticed he had a different Porsche; It was a black and silver Porsche Panamera. "You ready?"

I nodded my head and he held the door open for me; I slipped inside. I reached over and opened the door for him and he smiled. "That's why I put a ring on your finger."

"Uh hmm, I bet," I giggled. "You got a new car?"

He turned and looked at me. Placing his hand on my thigh and using his other hand to turn my face to him, I looked at him. His face got serious and I wondered what the hell he was going to say. "Peanut, I know you think I'm not concerned about the baby shi…stuff, but I am. I got this car for you because that's how much I believe that we'll have a kid one day." I looked in the back and there was a car seat.

"Zyair, you're crazy as hell," I smiled, trying to hold back the tears. I grabbed his face and placed a million kisses on his lips. "I love you so much for going out your way to make me smile, and make me feel better and secure in the decision. I have a truck already," I kissed him again, as he turned his hat to the back. Ugh, my fiancé was so damn fine.

"You can never have too many cars. This is your push present before you push. Just something to let you know that I'm thinking of us and we're on the same page."

Kissing him once more, I put my seat belt on. "Ugh, I love you too damn much right now."

"You better," he chuckled, and squeezed my thigh as we pulled out the parking lot.

We listened to music and sang along with different songs and talked about my day. I didn't really want to mention Blake coming in, so I didn't. We arrived at a little Italian restaurant in Williamsburg. I was glad that we didn't do anything major because I didn't feel like being bombarded by paparazzi. Once again, he opened the door for me and we walked the block to the restaurant. It felt good to just be on a date with Zyair and not Zane, the boxer. We didn't have valet, paparazzi or fans screaming for him. It was just me, him and our dinner. He held the door open and we were escorted to a private area in the corner. I slid into the booth and Zyair slid beside me, draping his arm around me.

"Welcome to Tony's, can I offer you guys something to drink… We also have a bar," the waiter pointed to the small bar in the corner.

"Yeah, let me get some Remy Martin and some water for the lady," He ordered for us, and I flipped through the menu. "Somebody wanna be pregnant so no drinks for you," he whispered in my ear, and kissed my forehead.

"It feels good to be out on a date. I feel like we're so busy that we never have time to spend with each other."

"I know; we gotta get better with that. I know you not gonna quit your job, but are you willing to slow your hours down?"

I sat silently for a minute. He wasn't asking me to quit my job and I was working twelve hour shifts about five days a week, so I could slow my workload a little bit and spend time with him. Relationships are all about compromise. I was so ready to tell him now, but I had to think about it.

"I can do that."

Kissing me on the cheek, he replied, "Good; I think we need to talk about some things."

"Okay…"

"Cabrina is on the cast of the new season of *Hollywood Exes*," he revealed, and I laughed.

"She's truly hilarious and relentless. I mean, that show is nothing but a bunch of desperate hoes talking about old dick they had. If she's happy, I'm ecstatic." I sipped my water, and squeezed my lemon into it.

He looked like he was relieved. "I thought you were going to go off."

"Not at all, but she needs to keep me out of anything." I had a plan for little Ms. Cabrina. She tried it with going to a reality show, but I was truly going to show her how it was to be schooled by the queen of petty town.

"I'm working with the lawyer to shut that down. We need to go sign those papers," he hinted at the prenup.

"I agree, make the appointment and we'll go."

We ordered our food, and I turned to face him a little more. "Moe, you gotta ease up on stressing yourself about wanting a baby. It'll happen, you need to believe that. To be real, this craziness got me second guessing shit," he honestly stated. I couldn't even be mad because I was going overboard, and he was speaking his truth.

"I know. I'm going to stop with all of that, I promise. We need to focus on us before worrying about trying for a baby. If it happens, we'll be good. I'm really enjoying this time with you." I rubbed his face and kissed him.

"That's my girl. It'll happen and when it does, we'll be happy. Right now, you gotta slow down with all your craziness."

"I agree," I giggled, and we kissed. "Now, where are we doing Thanksgiving?"

"We're doing it at our place. I'm going to have it catered this year."

I screwed my face up. "Uh huh, like Big Mama is going to have that. You better quit while your ahead," I joked.

"She's staying with us until after the new year," he blurted, and I choked on my water. He started patting my back, as I choked until tears came out my eyes.

"W…with us? Zyair, why didn't you tell me this?"

"I knew you would get crazy about it. You've been around Big Mama and you don't need to be doing all that overboard shit you be trying to do."

"Well, I don't want to be lazy either."

"You're far from lazy and she knows that. I think she's inviting Tammy's moms."

I shook my head because I knew that was nothing but a bad idea. Tammy couldn't stand surprises, and then to surprise her with a woman that continued to leave her high and dry was a recipe for disaster. "I don't think it's a good idea, but it isn't my choice."

"We're gonna be Kermit and sipping our tea. Ain't none of our business, but we'll be there for Tammy regardless."

"You're so damn crazy," I laughed, and we continued our date night. It felt so good to be out and about with my honey. I did need to stop with this baby making crap. We just got engaged and I was doing the most. From now on, I didn't plan to bring up the baby situation. I could tell in his face that I was doing entirely too much for him, and I never wanted him to feel that way. It didn't hurt to have fun making the baby, so that's what I planned on doing.

*

"Well damn, are you that hungry? Chewin' like a damn horse," Tammy snapped, as I ate my breakfast. I had an hour and a half until I had to get to work. I decided to invite Tammy to breakfast to catch up.

"Listen, I am starving and your cousin kept me up all night," I rolled my eyes and snickered.

She made a gagging sound and covered her mouth. "Now, you done wasted this food; I ain't even hungry anymore," she joked.

Zyair told me it was something that Tammy wanted to talk to me about, so I wasted no time in inviting her to breakfast before work. "You so stupid. What did you need to talk to me about?"

"Your man got a big ol' mouth. I told his ass that I was going to call you and invite you out. But anyways, I am pregnant," she revealed with a little smile on her face.

"Seriously?" I choked, while grabbing my water and guzzling it down. "So the IVF worked?"

"Yes, and I'm not surprised. I've always been a damn fertile myrtle. So, Rick has been misdiagnosed." She continued to lay the surprises out for me.

By now, I was literally choking with tears coming out my eyes. She came around the table and beat me on the back, while holding my arms up in the air. "I'm good, I'm good," I choked out. "How the hell did that happen? Didn't Zyair move him to another doctor?"

"Yep, but they didn't bother to do their research. Just decided to continue to do the same plan of treatment his other doctor was doing, but more aggressive."

"Oh my God, I can't believe that shit. You need to sue their asses for real," I shook my head shocked as hell.

"Zyair wants me to do the same thing. I'm just happy that he's going to be alright. My main focus is on him beating the cancer he does have. The new doctor said it's a chance, she's very hopeful."

I had tears falling down my cheeks, as I got up and hugged and kissed my best friend. "Tammy, I… I don't even know what to say."

"Get your emotional ass off of me," she giggled, and hugged me back.

"Alright, alright I am done. Guess who was up in the emergency room last night?"

She looked at me and waited for me to answer. "You know I hate guessing, who?"

"Blakeisha," I announced, and she laughed.

"First off, her mama need to be slapped with that damn name and secondly, what the hell was she in there for?"

"She's pregnant and having some issues. I had to be her damn nurse and then the bitch made me call Ki for her ass."

"Humph, couldn't be me. I would have ragged and tagged her ass out the damn bed. That shows growth on your part, babe." She smiled and squeezed my hand. "Let that been a couple months ago and your ass would have been calling me to pick you up from the police station."

"That shit doesn't even bother me anymore. Check this out, Cabrina is going to be on the new season of *Hollywood Exes*."

"Ewe, that bitch doesn't know when to quit." She turned her face up and rolled her eyes.

"Who you telling? Check this, I am about to be queen petty in this bitch."

"Please fill me in because I'm gonna be royal petty counselor," she snickered.

"Navi set an appointment with the same production company that films *Hollywood Exes*. You know I hate the media, but it ain't nothing to beat a bitch at her own game. I'm gonna meet with them about filming a wedding special for us. Talk whatever television company that is interested, to air it the same night her show premieres. Who you think they gonna watch?"

"Ahh, you a scandalous bitch, but I love it. What does Zyair think about it?"

"I don't know because I haven't spoke to him about it. Honestly, I don't care about his opinion because he's going to do it either way. Decking this bitch in her face each time I see her obviously hasn't worked, so I need to beat her at her fame whore ways."

"Damn, how did you think of that?"

"I had a comment on Instagram picture of me and Zyair. The fan suggested that I do it, so I'm gonna use her idea and do it. We're gonna donate all the money to charity, so they know it ain't about the money."

"I mean, I like the whole idea and the money will do some good, so I'm down."

"I have a meeting set up this weekend. Thankfully, I'm off and get to spend some time with my baby. He complained I work too much and need to fall back some."

"You do work a lot, Moe. It's not a bad thing, but you barely have time for yourself, so you def need to spend some time with your man. Y'all gonna be married soon on national TV," she laughed, and we clinked our orange juice.

We finished talking and catching up, then paid our check. We parted ways, and I got into my new Porsche and headed to work. Cabrina's ass was going to learn today, about messing with me and mine. I heard she was shopping for a spin off show about she and Zane's relationship. He said she still hit his phone up and blamed him for Hakeem firing her as his client. I dialed my house phone and waited for my mother to answer.

"About time I heard from you. I don't hear much from you girls since y'all moved out," she sassed into the phone.

"Sorry Mama. I've been working so much and barely have time to catch a nap and eat… How are you?"

"I'm doing good; that man of yours sent me to the spa yesterday," she beamed. I could tell she was smiling from the sound of her voice.

"Oh yeah? How was it?"

"Beautiful, Moe. I had mimosas and got my body rubbed down."

"I'm glad you had a good time, Mama. Where's Daddy…work?"

"You already know it. That man is due to retire in a couple months and hasn't slowed down yet. I don't know what he's going to do with all that free time once he finally retires," she laughed.

"Spend time with you and probably hit the golf course. Mama, I'm pulling into work right now. How about we go do dinner after work?" I offered.

"Sounds good. Have your sister bring my grandson along. I haven't heard from either of you lately… I miss y'all, that's all."

"Aww Mama, I miss you too. I'll call her on my lunch break and ask her."

"Alright, Moe," she said, and ended the call.

I parked in my regular spot and hopped out the car, grabbing my lunch bag. Just as I was closing my doors and about to press the alarm, Tanisha came out the hospital doors. I ignored her and hit my alarm and headed toward the hospital.

"He got you riding clean…You pregnant?" she questioned, looking at the car seat in the back. I forgot to take that out last night.

"He treats me nice, and that's none of your business." I turned on my heels and walked into the hospital.

I was tired of people thinking they could ask me these personal questions and expect me to answer it. Hell, this was my pussy and if I chose to disclose what was going in and coming out of it, it was my business. I didn't even like Tanisha, and she didn't like me, so why was she so comfy asking personal questions?

"Moet, I have you on the third floor today," my supervisor poked his head out his office and said. I didn't know why he kept moving me all these different places when he knew I liked to be in one place.

"Clarence, you know I ha-"

"I have enough of the nurses complaining. We're short staffed from the budget cuts, so you'll get on that third floor if you want to keep a job," he barked, and I rolled my eyes.

"Yeah, whatever," I mumbled, and went to clock in and start my shift.

I haven't been at work for an hour and I already had charts up to my neck. Since they were cutting hours, a lot of nurses were overworked and unappreciated, me included. I had to fill out charts, check patients, and do whatever else they decided to throw on my plate. I grabbed my first chart and almost threw it on my colleague's stack. Please believe if she wasn't sitting there, I would have. Blake's ass was like a thorn in my side that I couldn't reach. Shit, I thought they sent her ass home. I walked down the hall and into her room, and who do I find sitting in the visitor's chair with drool spilling from his lips? Ki's ol' nasty ass. Blake was sitting up and watching TV. She clicked the television off when I entered the room.

"How are you feeling, Ms. Brix?" I asked, as I went to check her vital signs.

"Moet, do you really have to be so formal?" she giggled, and my face remained the same.

"We're not friends, and I am professional, so it's Ms. Brix." I took her blood pressure, temperature and pulse.

"I'm still having a little pain, but the spotting has stopped."

"Uh huh, well I'll send someone in for some pain meds, but everything looks good." I grabbed the heart monitor machine and started moving it around to find the heartbeat. Once I found it, I turned up the machine so she could hear. "That's your little person's heartbeat," I offered a little smile.

"They're a little trooper," she smiled.

"Blake, I know you stay with a blunt and a beer; have you been doing that while pregnant?"

"Once I found out I was pregnant I haven't been doing that. I've been trying to eat healthy and do the right stuff…You know?"

"Alright, I'm gonna send someone in with some pain medicine in a few." I nodded, grabbed my chart and started to walk out the room.

"M…Moet?" I heard Ki stirring from his sleep. I looked back at him and shook my head, and headed out the room. What the hell did we have to speak about? Not a damn thing in my book.

"I know you hear me," he continued, and I turned around and looked at him. The fact that Blake was screaming at the top of her lungs for Ki to return to her room, Ki yelling for me to answer him, and my supervisor standing there with one of the board of directors of the hospital, didn't make for a good scene at all.

"Listen, I am at work right now. You need to lea-"

"What's going on, Nurse Rubbins?" Clarence asked, as he and the other visitor walked over to us.

"N…Nothing. I am explaining to the patient's boyfriend that-"

"Kion!!!!" Blake screamed from her room, and all I could do was bow my head.

"You know I don't love her at all and I want you," he continued his plead for my love. The fact that he didn't play along and continued to be selfish about his needs, when my job could potentially be on the line, pissed me off. It showed me that all he would ever care about is himself.

"Nurse Rubbins, can you please come to my office after you finish with this patient?"

"Sure," I said through clenched teeth, and turned on my heels.

Ki wasn't too far behind me, and another nurse had gone into the room to calm a screaming Blake down. The bitch was doing the most for a nigga that didn't give a damn about her.

"Listen, I am at work and we're as good as done. You never seem to surprise me; here you are with another chick that's pregnant, but you're trying to plea for my love. If you don't get out my face," I stated, and left him standing there.

After I put in Blake's medicine request, I went to Clarence's office. He was sitting there waiting for my ass too. I slipped in and closed the door behind myself, and sat down in the chair in front his desk.

"I don't know if it's because of your sister's accident or the fact that you're engaged to Zane Whitfield, but you have been off your game here at work," he started, and I immediately screwed my face up.

"Uh huh, don't do that, Clarence. Don't bring my personal business into this because it has nothing to do with it. I've been here on time and doing my job. If it was such an issue, I would have gone out with all the nurses that got laid off. My performance is impeccable and I am one of the top nurses in the running for chief of nurses. So, please don't insult me by bringing my personal business into this, because that is far from the issue," I schooled him, and crossed my legs.

"If that is so, why is your patient complaining about you openly flirting with her boyfriend?"

"Get the fuck outta here!" I yelled, almost in a crazed laugh. See, here is a lesson: never be nice to the snakes. Soon as you're nice, they come and bite your ass.

"Moet! Calm down! I know that's not true; why would you be flirting when you have a man of your own. However, the board wants to see some action done, so I am suspending you for two weeks."

"What? That's ridiculous!"

"I'm sorry, but hopefully you'll come back with a new attitude and will be ready to work professionally," he stated, as the board of directors stepped in the room.

I excused myself, and Clarence winked as I closed the door. I grabbed my stuff out of my locker and left the building. He said I could have finished my shift, but I knew if I went anywhere near Blake's room, I would be pissed and fuck her ass up – again.

As I was walking out the doors, I spotted Ki's dumb ass standing near the entrance of the hospital. Why couldn't he take a hint? I wasn't interested anymore, and the wool had been pulled from my eyes. I saw his ass for what he was and even if I wasn't with Zyair, I wanted nothing to do with him and his bullshit that seemed to follow.

"Get the fuck away from me and leave me alone, Kion," I snapped, and popped the locks to the car.

He quickly blocked the door and looked down at me. "Is this how it is now, Moe?"

"It's been like that, and you need to wake up and realize that we're done. I don't have time to be worrying about a nigga that's everybody's nigga. The sooner you realize that you lost a good one and another nigga picked her up, you'll be straight," I said, and shoved him out my way.

"It's real fucked up what you're doing, Moe. Throwing away a relationship, for what?"

"For love, commitment and matrimony. I'm getting all that from my man, and haven't gotten it from you and I've been in that relationship longer. Go to your baby mama." I hopped in my car and pulled off. Zyair was at the gym, so I went to the spa my mother told me about. I needed a little time to relax.

Monett

"Girls, I need you both to come around more often. What are you guys doing for the holidays?" my mother inquired, as she cuddled her grandson.

We were at dinner and enjoying some girl time. I hadn't caught up with Moet since she went off on me a couple days ago. Between being a mother, girlfriend and getting my shape back, I didn't have much time to kiss her ass anyway. I received a call from Johnathan the other day, and he wanted to set up visits with his son. I was still conflicted, and Hakeem's input didn't do anything but make it more confusing.

"Zyair and I are actually hosting dinner at our place. Of course, you guys are invited," Moet announced, as she poked around her steak.

"What's the matter, Moe?" I questioned. I noticed she had been withdrawn from the conversation.

"I got suspended from work because of Blake and Ki's messy asses."

"What? How?"

"I told you that girl is a damn mess… should have been cut that loose a long time ago," my mother sighed.

After she explained, I wanted to go see Blake's ass myself and give her these hands. How you still mad when she's not even with the nigga? I knew it was only so much she wanted to say with my mother around, so I didn't push her to speak about the situation any further.

"How are you and Hakeem, drama queen?" she joked, and I kicked her under the table.

"We're good, just trying to figure out time with a new baby and a new relationship. We're managing though."

"Just have patience and it'll all work out. Hakeem's a good boy and I could tell he wants this, so don't go acting all crazy," my mother warned.

"Too late," Moet snickered.

"Y'all got me running through y'all, so I know you can't help it. However, some good men have stepped into y'all lives, so keep that craziness to a minimum," she preached, and we laughed.

"I've been meaning to ask how's the situation with Johnathan and his family? Have they saw Nauti yet?"

"Nope, and I'm not ready for them to meet him yet. Johnathan has reached out, but I haven't given him a response yet. I'm still selfish with my baby," I said, as my mom handed him back to me and I kissed his fat cheeks.

"I can't believe he's going to be a month already," Moet squealed, and pinched his fat cheeks.

"It's going by so damn fast. What's going on with wedding preparations?"

"We're gonna get on those soon. I haven't had the time, but now with all this free time, I'll get to doing that."

"Let me know if you need any help. Me and Big Mama would love to help," my mother offered.

"I know, Mama. Right now, it's about me and Zyair's taste. You know how you can be, and let's not go there about Big Mama," we all giggled, because we knew it was true.

We ate dinner, gushed over Nauti, and caught each other up. We hadn't been out together in a while, so it felt good to talk and catch up with my sister and mother. Since my mother had to stop by my aunt's house, Moet decided to drive me home.

"What's with the car seat?" I questioned, and she laughed to herself.

"We're trying for a baby."

I coughed loudly and looked at her with wide eyes. "A baby? You're not even married yet," I pointed out, and she sucked her teeth.

"Monett, I don't see a ring on your finger. I don't have to be married to have a child, so don't come at me with that bullshit."

"You're right; don't you want to wait and enjoy your time together as a married couple first? I think a baby will complicate that."

"It's something to think about," she quietly replied.

"I heard about this Cabrina thing. How does that make you feel?" I heard from Hakeem that she was doing the show. I personally couldn't wait to tune in and see all the bullshit she was ready to tell the world. I knew my sister probably felt a way, so I didn't want to seem so eager.

"Girl, I got this whole plan down, and you're coming to the meeting," she informed me. Whatever she had in mind, I was going to be down regardless.

After she dropped me off, I struggled with the diaper bag and carrier into our apartment. Hakeem came out the office with the phone to his ear, and saw me struggling.

"I got you, ma," he said, and took the bag and Nauti from me. "Listen, I need him to be at the venue. I don't care about nothing else," he sternly stated into the phone and ended the call.

"Handling business as usual, huh?" I reached up and squeezed his cheeks, while placing a kiss on his lips.

"You already know… I'm trying to buy us that house in Long Island," he smirked and I kissed him again.

I loved that he always wanted to grind and make shit happen for us. As if this condo wasn't enough, he wanted to go bigger. We weren't the richest, but we had money and this was enough for me. Long as I was able to provide my son with a warm meal, bed and shelter, I was good.

"Babe, we don't need no big house in Long Island. Let me get him to bed and I'll make us something to eat."

He followed right behind me into Nauti's room, and plopped down on the rocker. "I want two big ass Rottweilers, so we gonna need a big crib for that. I want you to have everything you want and don't need."

I slipped my baby out his clothes and washed him with a warmed wipe. "Keem, we don't need all of that right now. I'm satisfied with us, this apartment and me waking up next to you every morning. A big house just means you'll be working and away from home more. Then where will that lead me? In a big ass house alone."

He rocked in the chair and looked through his phone. "I hear you, Monett. I'll chill right now, but I plan on getting a big ass house."

"Please chill," I giggled and kissed him, before returning back to the changing table.

"You looking real good," he licked his lips and came up behind me.

The only thing me and Hakeem did was kiss. Other than that, we never explored. It was like uncharted territory, and I was nervous. I really appreciated Hakeem taking his time with me, and waiting for me to deliver my son. Now, I was approaching that six-week mark and I was ready to rip his clothes off.

"You know I'm trying to get this body right and tight again," I blushed, as I lifted my fat baby boy.

I wasn't into the breastfeeding thing. I tried it out and realized it wasn't for me. I was working out, eating right and drinking this detox tea. A company on Instagram sent Moet a couple boxes to promote, but she claimed she didn't have time and wasn't about to be a walking billboard. I ended up using the tea and it was actually good, so they started sending it to me to promote. I was posting on Instagram and making a little bit of coins. Once I got this body in good shape, Moet promised she would hook me up with this photographer she knew.

"I see that, only thing you ain't losing is that big ass," he chuckled, and squeezed my ass, as I bent over to place Nauti in his crib.

I turned facing him, and wrapped my arms around his waist. "You're being fresh as hell right now."

"Hmm, you already know that's what I wanna be." He placed kisses on my neck, and gripped my ass.

"Keep it up, Keem," I flirted, and switched out the room.

I went into the kitchen and ordered us some food. I didn't have enough time to make a full dinner, and I was tired. Thankfully, we had a gym in the building and they had a nursery. I straightened up the house and did whatever dishes were in the sink before the delivery man came. I paid and tipped him and plated our food. Hakeem was in his office, so I brought our food in there and sat in the chair situated in front of his desk.

"Thank you, baby. I was thinking on taking a little weekend getaway this weekend," he suggested, looking up at me.

"Oh really? I don't know if I'm ready to leave Nauti alone for the weekend."

"C'mon, you need some time to be with your man. I already called Moet and she said she'll watch him."

"I feel like such a bad mother leaving him already. He's about to be a month, and I'm already going on weekend getaways," I sighed.

He came around his desk and wrapped his arms around me, while I sat in the chair. He placed small kisses on my neck. "Since he's been home, you've been spending all your time with him. You got out for the first time today, so yes, you need some time to be an adult. I'm thinking a hotel suite, some drinks and just some one-on-one time."

"Hmm, it doesn't sound too bad… Can I go shopping?"

"Of course; you know we gotta fuck up some commas for Nauti." He kissed me and returned to his seat.

"I'm liking this more and more. Alright, only over night though," I demanded.

"We can do overnight. We can leave Saturday and come back Sunday morning."

I got up and walked around his desk, before sitting down in his lap. I fed him a broccoli and kissed his lips. "Sounds like a deal to me."

After I finished dinner, I went down to the gym to get a little workout in, while Hakeem watched Nauti and got some work done before bed. I was in the middle of doing some squats, when my cell phone started ringing. I let it go to voicemail, but it started ringing soon after. I grabbed the phone and went to get on the treadmill.

"Yeah."

"It's Johnathan, how are you?" he asked, sounding quite pleasant. I guess getting clean was a good thing for him.

"I'm just working out while Nauti is sleeping."

"Oh. Who is watching him if you're working out?" he questioned, and I could almost hear the jealous tone of his voice.

"My boyfriend is watching him. What's up, Johnathan?" I asked, because I know he didn't call to shoot the breeze with me.

"I was calling to let you know that I'm done with my month in treatment program, and I'll be returning home this weekend. I still have to do meetings and shit, but for the most part, I am good and haven't touched a drink in almost a month. I want to see my son and spend some time with him this weekend," he slyly threw in.

Now, I didn't want to keep Johnathan out of my son's life at all. If that was the case, I would have let the police know what went on, and his ass would be in jail. Instead, I covered for his ass over and over again. When he beat my ass before I was pregnant and while I was pregnant, I still covered and didn't call the police. I don't know if he thought all of that was forgiven and we were about to be friends. My son was defenseless and I had to be his protector, so I was hesitant about my son going over there.

"Umm, I don't know about that, Johnathan. You can come over to my parents' house to see him before I go away for the weekend."

"You're going away for a weekend, but I can't take him for the weekend? My family has been reaching out to you to see him and you've ignored them," he ranted, and I ran my hand through my hair and admired my body.

"Listen, your parents didn't return my calls when I reached out to them, when I needed them to speak to you. So yes, I've been ignoring their calls because I am not going all the way to Staten Island with a new baby. There isn't anything wrong with their feet, so if they want to see Nauti, then they need to come see him at my parents' house."

"You still going off that? I th-"

"Whatever you are about to say, you thought wrong. I'm happy you are finally getting clean and getting whatever help you needed from day one, but that doesn't change the fact that you've beat me, and then tried to kill me and your son. You know I hate drama, which is the reason why I kept this between us. I believe people can change, so that's why you're in a treatment center and not in someone's prison."

"Aright, I have to go… I'll call you once I get back in New York."

I ended the call without saying another word. He pissed me off thinking I was supposed to wipe all this under the rug and act like he's been supportive and nice all this time. He's been a monster straight from hell, but I still decided to be nice about the situation and still be the light in his dark ass life. Soon as you involve my son, that bright light quickly turned dark. Johnathan had a lot of proving to do before I let him walk to the next room with my son. I finished my workout and went upstairs to get some sleep before my son woke me up to eat.

Moet

"Aye, you need to stop with that snoring at night. How the hell a nigga supposed to sleep?" Zyair called from the bathroom, with his toothbrush still in his mouth.

"Boy please, you're the one grinding your teeth and talking in your sleep. You need to find Addy, because I am tired of you calling out to her every night," I smacked my gums, and finished applying the makeup to my face.

"Don't play like that, Moe. Addy was my first dog, that shit still hurt," he griped, and I laughed at his silly ass.

"Well, go get you another one and name her Addy, so you can shut the hell up. Talking 'bout me but screaming for a damn dog." I puckered my lips and slathered some MAC lipstick over them.

He washed his mouth out, and turned the faucet on his side off. "Where you going all dolled up?" Looking down at his attire, which was gym clothes he said, "I know my ass ain't going, so where you going?"

I walked over to him and rubbed his washboard abs, and reached up to kiss him. He was so damn fine, and every day I still couldn't believe that he was mine. Y'all probably thought I was done with him after that Cabrina madness, but nope. That's exactly what she wanted and I was going to give it to her. The best revenge was getting my mind right and making it work with Zyair.

"Those kisses are nice and shit, but where you going?" he continued to probe, but I wasn't answering. How was I going to tell him that I was going to meet with a company about our reality show?

"I just want to look nice to pick myself up from being suspended from work. All week I lounged around in pajamas, and now I want to look good."

"I smell bullshit, Moet," he looked at me, and I busied myself with looking for a purse to wear. I had a few things the designer dropped off, but I had to seriously organize my things in this closet. Half of my stuff wasn't even put away, and I felt I didn't have enough to fill my whole closet.

"Babe, I smell your cologne, not shit… Come home early and we'll do dinner. I'm gonna cook and massage your body and you might get some," I winked, kissed him and headed out the door.

I planned to do all those things because I was hopeful that I would get the show. I had to butter him up one way or another, but I knew I was going to throw up what happened with Cabrina, so I would get my way either way.

A car was already waiting for me once I got outside. A couple paparazzi were already waiting, but nothing major. The building had forbidden them to hang out in front the building. There were a bunch of celebrities in that building as well, and they wanted to protect their residents. Monett was going out of town tomorrow, so she wanted me to watch Nauti. I told her I would, but only if she came with me to the meeting. I invited Tammy, and she was on her way too. Monett was picking her up, and they were meeting me at the restaurant. I snapped a few selfies and closed my phone. I answered my ringing cell phone, and looked out the window; we were nearing the restaurant.

"Where the hell you at?" Tammy's loud ass mouth came through the phone receiver.

"I'm pulling up now… Where you at?"

"Sitting outside the restaurant, and I'm hungry," she replied.

I ended the call because we pulled right in front where she and Monett were standing. The driver opened the door and I stepped out, adjusting my skirt. "Damn, it's freezing out here. Why y'all waiting outside?" I asked, as we walked inside.

"Heifer, my man got money, but he ain't balling like this," Tammy was the first to speak, and I fell out laughing. She was the first to let you know what her ass could and couldn't afford.

"The people we're meeting is going to foot the bill. Hell, they better or Zyair's gonna think I was having an expensive dinner with someone else."

We took a seat and waited for the producers to come. That gave us a little time to have some girl talk. All three of us hadn't hung out in a while, and I know Monett didn't know about Tammy's pregnancy and Rick's new hopeful lease on life. While we were chatting, a white woman and black man came and sat down on the other side of the table.

"How are you doing Ms. Rubbins?" The man extended his hand and I shook it.

"I'm fine, how are you?"

"That's good to hear. Your assistant said you requested a meeting. She said you had something we might be interested in," the woman stated, getting right to the point.

"Well damn, she ain't even get water before she got to the point," Tammy whispered in my ear, and I shook her off.

"Well, I am interested in doing a wedding special on your network." I closed my menu and looked at the waiter. "Send us some wine, and a side salad for her, please."

"Bitch, I don't want no damn sala-"

"Tammy," I said lowly, while gripping her leg.

"We've done plenty of wedding specials, and would love to host yours. However, things need to make sense financially. What are you guys talking?"

"Actually, we would like all our earnings to go to a charity or charities of our choosing."

Once I said that, I got them interested and leaning closer, and the table wasn't even that big. "Zane Whitfield has never been on any reality shows. Definitely would be something different and we can get the viewers. Everyone wants to know what the rowdy chick that's on his arm is like," the white woman said to the man, as he pondered the decision.

"Would you be interested in doing a whole show, instead of just a special?" the man questioned, and I shook my head.

"Absolutely not; we're just interested in everyone seeing our love on the TV screen. Now, another thing I would need is to make the premiere date February 14th," I added.

The woman flipped her iPhone out and started looking through her calendar. When it all added up to her, she smiled at me with a wide tooth grin. "That is the day *Hollywood Exes* premieres on VH1."

"Exactly, how about we see who gets the most views?"

"Is it just the wedding or everything leading up to it?" the male asked. It was obvious he was trying to rank in more cash for the network. He knew if he got us to sign on for our own season, that meant more money, views and ratings for the network.

"I'm a very private person, so I would like to do just the wedding. I don't need everything leading up to it. I'll tell you what, for the bachelorette party, you can film that."

"Deal, we'll get the contracts drawn up and sent over to you. Just have Zane sign them, and we'll be ready for filming when the bachelorette party comes and the wedding following."

I stood up and shook both of their hands. "Thank you, I appreciate the time and opportunity."

"No, thank you. This a genius media opportunity, and we'll need to get some promo shoots so we can get the commercial together." The man stood up and shook my hand.

"I know that's not my boo, Moet," I heard, and turned around and saw Matt sitting with two gorgeous women. I ran over to him and gave him a hug, as he looked me over.

"How are you, boo?" I said, hugging him again.

"You know I'm good, but I see you're better. I've been holding on to those photos and I'm dying to release them," he snapped, and I laughed.

"I might have a reason for you to release them very soon. You know I'll keep you posted," I told him, thinking of the wedding special.

He looked around me, and slapped his hands down on his legs. "You didn't tell me you had a twin…" His voice trailed off, as he walked around Monett like we weren't in a restaurant – a five-star one at that.

"She's not my twin, she's my older sister and I told you about her. She's into modeling and I want you to shoot with her."

"Yass! She's gorgeous and I would love to. I know a couple people at a few magazines, and I could probably get you in some. Now, I don't know about the cover yet, but baby, with that face you'll get there."

"I love modeling; I used to stay in the mirror practicing as a child… I just had a baby though," she revealed, and he laughed.

"Through a surrogate? I damn sure don't see a baby coming out that little tight body. Listen boo, we'll start slow and then I'll get you where you need to be. Look, I'm in New York for a couple months working at *Complex* magazine, so we can have some lunch and discuss some stuff."

"Matty, I'm gonna need a wedding photographer. We haven't taken any pictures yet, and we need engagement phot-"

"Boo, you don't need to ask twice. Call me and we'll get that done," he hugged me. One of the girls he was with sucked her teeth, so he turned his attention to her. "Girl, don't do it, please. I'm doing you a fav-"

"What the hell am I, chopped liver?" Tammy blurted and he laughed.

"Baby, chopped liver gets eaten too… how you doing, I'm Matt," he hugged her, and she laughed.

"Boo, just call me and we'll do some lunch together and discuss some stuff. Call me, and catch up. Oh, and I need to get you out in these clubs," he hugged me, and I laughed. Zane wasn't about to let me in no club without him.

We left the restaurant and decided to do some retail therapy. While we were shopping, Tammy filled Monett in on what had been going, and of course she got emotional. Hell, I did too. We continued to shop until I looked at the time, and realized I needed to be home getting ready for tonight. I kissed my girls and headed my ass home, because I knew I had to do a lot in order to convince Zyair this was a good idea.

*

I sat on the kitchen stool with dinner waiting, and my notepad. Thanksgiving was next week, and I had to get this list together for Big Mama. She called everyday to add more stuff I needed to get on it. Man, that woman could talk your ear off, but she was so sweet. I heard the door chime, and abandoned the stool, and stood near the stove with this red crotch-less lingerie I was wearing. Yeah, it was doing too much, but I had to be convincing and men are physical beings.

"Baby, where you at?" he called until he found me in the kitchen. He dropped his gym bag and leaned on the wall. "Damn, we doing it like that now?" he smirked, and took his shirt off, but I had to stop him.

"Oh no, Papi gotta eat so he'll be well energized for tonight," I cooed, and he grabbed the throbbing member in his pants. "Let me feed you, Papi," I continued to play my role.

Men loved to feel like they're in control, even when their not. Zyair knew I would fuck him and whoever up and I didn't play games, but tonight, he was in control. I was being submissive to him, and in his little man brain, he was calling the shots. Hell, I'll let him think that for tonight, but he knew when that alarm rang tomorrow, I was back to running shit.

"Peanut, that shit is sexy as fuck. Your ass needs to be suspended from work more often." He licked his lips before kissing me on the lips.

Rubbing his shoulders, as he scooped the rasta pasta in his mouth, he was in heaven. He had a bad bitch rubbing him down, food, and he just knew the night was gonna end with some pussy.

"So baby, I got some news for us," I started, and he stopped eating and turned to look at me, but I turned his head to focus on his food. "Eat your food, Papi."

"You pregnant?" he asked, and it sounded like he was excited. I was a little disappointed that I was telling him no.

"No, babe," I rubbed his shoulder again. I placed kisses on his neck and arms, as he finished eating.

"It'll happen, don't go getting all sad and suicidal on me and shit."

I laughed and shook my head. "We're doing a wedding special with Bravo," I blurted, and tried to kiss his arms, but he jumped out the stool, knocking over his bowl.

"What the hell you just say, Moet?"

I stood in front of him and placed my hands on my hips trying to distract him, but he wasn't trying to see or hear any of that. "Put that robe on, and repeat what you just said." He threw me the robe, and I put it on.

"We're doing a wedding special," I mumbled, and he slapped the counter.

"For what? Why the fuck we need people in our business? We're not hurting for money!" he yelled.

"Babe, calm down. We're donating the money to charity, so don't worry about that."

"Moet, tell me a reason why we need to be doing this. I ain't signing shit, and you'll be on there marrying your damn self!" he hollered, and I rolled my eyes.

"I'm tired of your old bitch fucking with me! Bad enough she has pictures floating around with her and you together, but now she's on a show. I'm tired of it and this is how I'm gonna shut her up!" I screamed and pushed the vase on the floor. I knew the shit cost like four thousand dollars, but I didn't give a damn.

"Man, you need to be the big-"

"Don't fucking tell me to be the bigger person, because the Lord himself knows that's what I've been doing. I've tried being the bigger person and ignoring this bitch, especially when she tagged me in a disrespectful post. I've tried to be the bigger person when it came to Blake, and I've tried to be the bigger person when it came to Ki. I'm tired of being the bigger person because that shit is working out in everyone's favor but mine!" I stomped out the room, and slammed the bedroom door closed. I even locked that shit, and got into the bed.

He wants me to continue being the bigger person, but everyone around me was being childish. Yeah, two wrongs don't make a right, but shit, I was tired of being right and then end up being done wrong. This is the one thing that I want to happen, but he doesn't want do it. I've sat and been the little quiet polished chick that he's asked for. I haven't decked a bitch in a while, and I ask him to do one thing and he can't do it. Fuck that!

"Open the door, Peanut," he knocked on the door, but I put the covers over my head and closed my eyes. His ass would be standing out there all night, so his best bet was to go and get a blanket and head to one of the spare bedrooms. I closed my eyes and was out a couple minutes later.

Zane

"Fuckin' back hurting and shit," I mumbled, as I got off the couch and heard Moet smacking on some breakfast. I didn't expect her ass to leave me locked out the bedroom, so I sat on the couch and waited for her to cool off. Well, I saw she wasn't playing, because my ass just woke up with all different types of crooks in my neck and back. "Good morning," I said, but she turned her nose up at me and continued eating.

She had a full spread of breakfast in front of her, and left not a damn thing for me. I grumbled and poured myself a bowl of cereal, and set my bowl in front of her. I looked at her, but she pretended I wasn't even in the room. I was pissed that she wanted to do this show, but she was my baby, so I was gonna do it for her. I wanted her to be happy and get this little revenge she'd been wanting to get on Cabrina's ass. My cell phone rang and she wasn't that mad that her ass couldn't scan my call. Speaking of the damn devil, I was about to ignore it, but Moet answered.

"Can I help you, hoe?" she laughed into the phone, and bit into a piece of bacon, while putting it on speaker.

"I'm the hoe, but you're sleeping with my man and took my man. Bitch please!" Cabrina yelled, and Moet was tickled.

"He wasn't that much of your man if I took him, right? He's my damn man and you're gonna learn real soon about that. I've been letting your ass get away with a lot, but soon as he becomes my husband, these calls and little games you're playing will be dealt with," she spoke, snapping her neck and all kinds of shit.

"H-" I didn't get to hear what Cabrina was about to say because she ended the call and blocked her number. She put her plate in the sink and then walked away.

"I thought you weren't talking to me?" I called behind her, and she continued walking to the back.

"I'm not… Change that number or we're going to have another issue, selfish ass," she mumbled, and I chuckled.

"I heard that!"

"It was meant for your big ass ears to hear," she shot back and slammed the door.

I finished my breakfast and went to go in the room, but she had it locked again. I knew I had to tell her that we could do this, or I wouldn't have a peaceful house, and I couldn't sleep outside my room another night. Her father warned me that his girls were used to getting their way, so I had to get used to caving in a lot.

"Can I come in?" I knocked on the door, and she opened the door, while throwing the lingerie in the hamper. Man, I wished I could have had my way with her last night, while she had that shit on.

"Grab what you need and continue out the room, please," she snapped, as she pulled some clothes out of shopping bags.

"Damn Peanut, we can do the show… Why you being so damn mean?" I plopped on the bed and started making snow angels in it.

"I'm tired of doing what you want. A relationship is compromise and that is what you are not doing." She folded clothes and placed them neatly on the bed.

"I said we can do the show; you really need to go on with this speech?"

"Uhh, yeah, because you seem to think you're the most important. It's nice that you're willing to do the show, after I had to lock you out the bedroom and ignore you. I shouldn't have to do all of that." She folded her arms, and I got off the bed and wrapped my arms around her.

"You're right; you also need to stop doing shit without me. How do you know this is something I wanted to do?"

"I knew you wouldn't want to do, but that didn't matter. Cabrina's ass is embarrassing me and I want to shut her ass up."

"You're giving her the power. If you ignore her than you wouldn't be giving a fuck about what she's doing. Moe, you give people too much control when you care."

I could tell she thought what I said was true, because her loud ass mouth was quiet for once. She hugged me and looked up at me. "I'm just tired of everyone coming for me. Whether it's Cabrina, Blake or Ki. I need to do this so they can all see this relationship isn't a joke, and it's real."

I chuckled and kissed her. I could tell she was trying to go about this with another approach. Let this had been a couple months, hell weeks ago, and she would have been beating the shit out of Blake in the hospital, and heading to Cali to whip Cabrina's ass, so I saw the growth.

"I'm not going to the gym, so I want to spend the whole day together."

She smirked and dropped down to her knees. She took my boxers down, and my member was already at attention. Moet could tap me, and my dick automatically got hard. Imagine what my shit was doing while she was stroking and spitting on my shit. Yeah, this shit was as hard as memorizing the bible in Spanish. Her mouth was so warm as she welcomed me into her mouth. Damn, that job she was doing was a hell of a job, and had me holding her head. She deep throated my shit a few times, and my toes was curling. Damn, who knew my future wife had a fire head game. She continued sucking my shit hard and playing with my balls, as I held her head.

"Damn Moe, shit," I moaned, and she kept going, tickling my shit with her tonsils. When she made a popping noise with her mouth, it was over. I tried to move her so I could nut, but she kept her mouth glued to my shit, as I released into her mouth. She swallowed the shit and got off her knees with a smirk.

"Now what were you saying?" She pulled her hair out the ponytail and walked into the bathroom. Nah, she wasn't about to get away with this shit.

I came up behind her and snatched down her leggings. She gasped, and tried to pull them up, but I slapped her hands. I pulled apart those fat ass cheeks and slipped right inside her. I pulled on her ponytail and blew in her ear. She hated when I did that because it made her wet. When I heard her shit get gushy, I pushed her head forward and slammed my shit right into her. She was moaning and screaming my name. All that cocky shit she was trying to do, failed horribly. She knew what time it was when I whipped my shit out.

"You love me?"

"Yes, you know I do…" she moaned, and threw that shit back on me. I dunked her shit like I was Michael Jordan in a game in '92.

I felt myself tighten my grip on her hips, and slammed myself inside one more time, before I came inside her. Her juices came down my leg as I kissed her on the neck.

"Now, stop acting like you run shit," I said and slapped her ass. "Come shower because we need to go to the lawyer's office."

*

On the ride over, I noticed she was quiet. I figured she was in her own thoughts, but she ain't say anything during our ride to Long Island. I touched her thigh and she offered a weak smile. Now I knew something was wrong. Why y'all women had to be so damn difficult?

"What's good with you, Peanut?" She shrugged her shoulders and continued looking out the window. "Moet, keep it a hundred with me, for real. None of that kiddie shit."

"Do you trust me? Do you think I would do you like that?" I had to look at her and then return my eyes back to the road.

"What the hell you talking about? I just fucked you bare back in our bathroom. If that ain't trust enough, I don't know what is."

"So why are we signing a prenup? I know my daddy didn't make my mama do one."

"Yo' daddy didn't have over four-hundred million in the bank. I thought we discussed this and you were cool with it?" I replied.

"I thought it was a little test or something. I didn't think we would actually be doing one. I don't care about your money, but signing a contract basically stating we're going to break up, is basically like cursing our marriage from jump."

"I feel you, but it's to protect u-"

"Nah, it's to protect you!" she snapped, and crossed her arms.

I loved Moet a lot, and I had a lot of patience with her. Yet, this was millions of dollars she could inherit if I died, or we divorced. My family was always to be taken care of before anything else. Moet wasn't like that, but when you are heartbroken, going through a divorce and dealing with lawyers, ain't no telling how you would be.

"Baby, it ain't even like that. Stop making something out of nothing."

"I'm cool, let's sign this so we can be straight." She brushed me off, and I continued to drive.

Her little attitude was out of control, but I knew that walking into this. Her father warned my ass, too, and I still leaped into this shit. No matter how much I dicked her ass down and showed her who was boss, her ass still wore the pants. I pulled into the parking lot and we walked inside. They were already waiting, so they took us to the conference room. I tried to grab Moet's hand, but she snatched it back. I snatched that shit back and put in my pants.

"Zyair, you're so damn nasty," she muttered, and tried to snatch her hand back. I pulled her chair out and then sat down.

"Hello Mr. Whitfield… We're here to sign the prenuptial agreement. Ms. Rubbins, we'll go over everything and agree to the terms, okay?" a white woman said, touching Moet's shoulder.

"Um, who are you?"

"I'm your lawyer, Ms. Rubbins. I'm here to make sure you're protected in this agreement."

She looked at me and I smirked, while sitting back in my chair. "Slick ass," she whispered in my ear.

Of course I wouldn't leave my baby blind. As my wife, she was entitled to every and anything I had. However, once those rings slipped off her fingers and the ink on the papers dried, I wanted to make sure my shit was safe.

"Are we ready to discuss the terms?" My lawyer looked around and everyone nodded. "Okay, so this is gonna be pretty simple. Everything that Mr. Whitfield has occurred before the marriage will be his, if you both happen to divorce. In the event of a divorce, Moet Rubbins will leave the marriage with 5.5 million dollars, the house in Miami and their penthouse in New York. Mr. Whitfield will pay for all the upkeep on each residence, along with the Rolls Royce, Mercedes and all the things that were gifted to her during the marriage."

She looked at me and wiped the tears in her eyes. She leaned over and whispered into her lawyer's ear. "Well, Ms. Rubbins said this isn't necessary. She'll just take her car if they divorced."

"This is the agreement, Peanut. Together or not, I'm always gonna look out for you, babe. Come here," I called her, and she came and sat on my lap, and buried her face into my shoulder as I rubbed her back. She was so damn emotional, but I loved her crazy ass.

"Is she going to sign?"

"Of course." I took the paper and put my John Hancock on the dotted line. Moet did the same, and we finished. I grabbed her hand, and we left and leaned on the car.

"Baby, I really don't need all of those things."

"Ma, I got you, so knock all that off. Let's go shopping so you can fill that closet," I kissed her, and helped her in the car.

Chapter Six

Tammy

"I know one damn thing, if that bitch knock on my door, I'm gon' slap her ass into next week, or whatever crack house she'll be in by next week!" I screamed, as Rick tried to calm me down. My mother had the damn nerve to come knock on my damn door, demanding that I allow her to see my child.

"Calm down, Tam," Rick said, rubbing my back, but I was far beyond calm. This bitch really thought I was going to allow her to just pop back in my life. Hell to the damn no! She couldn't be bothered when I was a child and needed her the most. But now that I had my shit half together, she wanted to come snoop her little dope head out ass in my door.

"She got some damn nerve coming to knock on my door. Let a crack head knock on my door, and I'm going to knock her teeth out personally!" I continued to yell, as I slammed around pots and pans.

I was pissed for two reasons: I planned lunch with just me and Rick and was planning on telling him about me being pregnant. Once I got lunch on the table, this bitch comes knocking on the door demanding shit. Now, not only was the lunch ruined, but so was my surprise. I couldn't even fake excitement with what this bitch just did.

"That shit ain't even good for the baby… Calm your ass down," Rick demanded, as he got out the seat and walked over to me.

Yeah, you heard me right. My man was walking over to me, and I was so damn happy. He hadn't started his bone treatments yet, but he was back on chemo and it was making a big difference.

"How…How did you know?" I stuttered, and tried to busy myself with dishes, but his ass stopped me and turned me around.

"You think I don't go in the medicine cabinet. My question is why did you try and hide this from me, Tamala?"

"I'm not; I was actually about to tell you before this bi-"

"That's your mother, Tam. Stop calling her everything but that. Eventually, you're going to have to have a discussion with her."

I folded my arms and squinted my eyes at him. "You're out your mind if you think I'm going to talk to her. Let me make sure I overdose your ass when I give you your medicine."

"Dion deserves to know both her grandparents. You need to let her make the decision if she wants her grandmother in her life. Your mother has done some fucked up shit, but she's trying to be better. Let her prove you wrong before you shut her down."

"Whatever, Rick. When did you become this second-chance giver?"

"Don't matter. You need to stop being such a mean ass and let those walls down." He walked slowly back to his room. He still stayed downstairs because he did get easily winded and he still had oxygen. I didn't want to push him too much. "Stop upsetting my damn baby in your stomach. Calm your ass down!" he yelled, and I rolled my eyes.

"Give a man a new lease on life and he's bossing you around," I mumbled, and got his lunch together. Dion was sitting in her high chair, watching me and her crazy daddy go back and forth.

After I gave Rick his lunch and got Dion down for a nap, I decided to call my cousin. I hadn't heard from him since I told him about Rick. Rick said he stopped by a couple times when I was gone. Thanksgiving is next week, and I needed to know if he wanted me to cook. Plus, I didn't know who was getting Big Mama from the airplane hanger. She couldn't stand to be chauffeured alone, so I knew a familiar face had to go pick her up.

"What's good, lemon head?" he grunted, and I laughed. He hadn't called me that since I was a child. I was in love with lemon heads and ate them faithfully as a child. Give me twenty-five cents and I'll come back with a box of lemon heads and a smile.

"I got some free time and wanted to chop it up with you…What you doing?"

It sounded like he was at the gym, so I knew Moet wasn't anywhere near him. "At the gym trying to get this work out in before I pig out for Thanksgiving. Big Mama is coming in Monday night," he revealed, and I sighed.

"When the hell were you going to call me and tell me?"

"Relax, Moet is going to pick her up and bring her back to our crib. But, you know she's gonna want to come by your place."

"Ugh, I don't feel like telling her my business. I think Rick has an-"

"Bullshit, Tammy. You need to spend some time with Big Mama. You know she feels like you've been closed off since the Rick shit."

"That's because she's always telling my business to my mother," I snapped, upset that he was taking her side. I loved Big Mama, but that old lady knew how to pull on someone's heart strings, like she was innocent.

"How you figure?"

"The bitch just left a few minutes ago, demanding that I let her see her grandchild, and help her out since Rick is sick. Who else told her that shit?"

"Man, I ain't spoke to your moms since she conned me out of thirty thousand for that damn rehab. I get how you feel, but you know Big Mama the verbal New York Times."

"Well, I'm 'bout to be the damn judge and shut down her shit. Anyways, what is going on with you?" I switched subjects before I got upset all over again.

"Moet done signed us up for some wedding special reality show. I don't even want to do this shit, I ain't for the reality life," he sighed.

"Well, you know Moet ain't like that either, but these hoes have pushed her ass to this. Once this is over and done with, she'll be over this feeling of having something to prove."

"Shit, I hope. She locked a nigga out the room and caught an attitude when I told her we couldn't do it."

I laughed so hard that I started choking. "You know her and Monett spoiled as hell. Their daddy spoiled their asses rotten, so any man that's gonna step into their life gotta be prepared for that. You see their mama; their daddy still spoils her. She's the only heifer I know that don't have to work because she's got diabetes," I laughed, and Zyair started cracking up.

"You ain't shit, you know that?"

"So I've been told. Moet is a good girl that's been through her share of deadbeat niggas. She's never had that stay and fight relationship, which still surprises me that y'all are engaged and about to be married. Every nigga that she has dealt with, and it's only a few, have done her wrong. They have her thinking she's wifey, while they're out with the next bitch. So with Cabrina, she has something to prove and so do you. Yeah, severing business ties was big on your part. However, you need to publicly embarrass that bitch, because that's what she's trying to do with you by going on this show."

I could tell he was absorbing everything I was saying. Let a bitch fuck with Rick and my relationship like that bitch had done to Moet and Zyair's, and I would have personally beat that bitch's ass.

"I hear you, cuz. We're doing the show, so I'm back in the room now," he laughed, and I joined him.

"Just make her happy, and always make her feel secure. Now, for the wedding special, you know a bitch gotta get done up to get on TV."

"You so damn crazy," he laughed in the phone.

"Uh huh. Me and Rick has another appointment. The treatments have been working, but you know he's not out the woods yet."

"Yeah, I know. That doctor is the best oncologist in the country, so I have faith. We filed that lawsuit, so it's only a matter of time before we hear anything."

"Alright, I just want that to be over with, so we can focus on him being good."

"Yeah, I know…" his voice trailed off.

"So, call me later and tell me when Big Mama comes."

"Fo' sure." We ended the call, and I went to take a quick nap before Rick's appointment.

*

"Yo' mama need to stop snatching my damn baby out my arms. Next time I'm gonna shift her damn wig," I vented, as Rick looked at the television in the waiting room. I could tell he was nervous, and I was a little too. That's probably why I threatened to shift his mama's wig.

Dr. Hanna had called us in to speak with us about something. I was nervous because as far as I knew, everything was good. My husband was going to beat cancer, but it was far from that. Although his cancer wasn't as advanced as we thought, the truth of the matter was that he still had cancer. She said she wanted to do a couple more tests and look everything through thoroughly. Now she was calling us back only a week into chemo, and I was scared. Rick grabbed my hands and looked into my eyes, offering a weak smile.

He knew when I got quiet I was thinking and worrying too much. This shit was too damn much and I didn't want to deal with this anymore. I just wanted to get a magic potion that would make the cancer go away.

"Mr. and Mrs. Smith," the nurse called, and I helped Rick up and we walked to the back. I was about to go in the exam room, but the nurse led us to the office. Since Dr. Hanna was a doctor in Alaska, she had to get privileges in New York just to treat Rick.

We both sat down and held hands, as we waited for the doctor. My leg kept shaking, so I had to cross it to contain it. I felt like I was in the principal's office about to get in trouble. I didn't know what the hell to expect, and I didn't know if my heart could take it anymore. The door opened, and in walked Dr. Hanna. I would have thought she would have got some color, but her ass was still pale as hell.

She took a seat and placed the papers and files she had in her hands down. "How are you guys doing? Every patient I had today has been complaining about the weather, and I laugh. I tell them they haven't had a winter until they lived in Alaska," she chuckled, and arranged the files on the desk.

I could tell the desk was another doctor's since it was a picture of a young woman with big breasts, and two little bad ass boys. "We're doing good, Doc. What did you need us to come in for?" Rick answered, getting straight to the point.

"Straight to the point, huh?" she smiled, and pulled out an X-ray. "You have some tumors that are pressing on your nerves and tissues. I want to go in and remove it all, but there is a procedure called limb salvage surgery, where I can remove the part of the bone with cancer. Then I'll put a metallic implant to replace the portion of the bone that was removed."

"So will the cancer be gone?"

"I can't say right now, but before we get to that point, we want to monitor and do radiation to try and shrink it. If that doesn't work, we'll do the surgery. We're almost out the woods, calm down," she offered me a smile, and I sighed a breath of relief.

"Here I thought he had a damn flesh eating disease and the cancer done formed a conjoint twin and shit," I sighed, and she giggled.

"Your wife is something else, Mr. Smith."

"Don't I know it," he laughed and squeezed my thigh.

We talked and discussed more treatment plans and confirmed them. She gave a deadline by January 15th that if it hadn't shrunk, she was going to go forth with the surgery, and we were excited. We left the office holding hands, and went to have some dinner before going to pick Dion up. It felt like old times between us, and I couldn't wait for many, many more.

Monett

I walked around the room and looked out the window. When he said just a night away, I didn't think he meant a night in Vegas. He booked a suite in the MGM and had everything laid out. I missed my baby so much and couldn't stop thinking about his little self. Then again, I didn't want to continue bringing it up to Hakeem. I knew he didn't mind, because Moet had sent us a picture of him, and he was more into the picture than I was. I gave her strict instruction that if Johnathan showed up at my house, he wasn't allowed to see the baby without me there. Since our little disagreement the other day, I hadn't heard from him. In a way, I was a little happy because I didn't feel like dealing with him right now.

"What you thinking?" Hakeem whispered in my ear, as he wrapped his arms around my waist. I looked up at him, and looked at the sun setting over Vegas.

"This is so beautiful and different. Last time we were here, I was pregnant," I smiled.

"Nah, the last time I was here, I met the most beautiful and slightly rude woman." I turned toward him and looked up at him.

"I was not mean to you. You just kept asking me if I was alright, and I was fine," I defended my self, and he smirked.

"Nah, I remember you being hella mean. It's alright though, you my baby now so we're good."

He opened the balcony and we both stepped out and felt the air blowing. The sky was a burnt orange, as we looked out into the sky. It felt so good to be in a man's arms that really cared about me. I felt so safe, beautiful and loved when I was around Hakeem. My parents always told both Moet and I when we found that one, we would know. I definitely knew, and was excited to see where our future would go.

Kissing me on the neck, he said into my ear, "I have dinner reservations for us, so I'm gonna need you to get yourself dressed. Let me see that body you've been working so hard on."

"What else do you have up your sleeve?" I giggled, and wiggled my way out his grip.

I couldn't lie and say I wasn't nervous about having sex with Hakeem. Tonight, I was going to give him some. I was ready and willing to give myself to him. In a weird way, I felt like a virgin going through this. In a sense, I was kind of a virgin with him.

"Oh, I got a lot of plans for us tonight. I want to wine and dine you, and make sure I take care of all your needs. You've been handling Nauti, the house, and making sure we're all good, that you need a minute to be catered to."

"Well then, I better go get dressed." I kissed him, and went off to the bedroom.

After a shower, doing my makeup and curling my hair, I was ready to go. I dressed in a burgundy bondage dress, a pair of nude strappy heels, and a matching clutch. I spiral curled my hair into big bouncy curls that hung down my back. Before we left, I went to go get my bundles put right back in. I put a little Chanel perfume on and stepped out the room. Hakeem was in the middle of a phone call, but ended the call as soon as he laid eyes on me. My baby was rocking a Burberry shirt, jeans and a pair of loafers. I could smell his cologne from across the room and he hadn't even made it to me yet.

"Hmm, damn the gym doing that body good," he complimented and spun me around.

I smiled and did a little dance and let him rub my ass. "I got to keep this body tight," I blushed.

"Shit, I'm gonna have fun showboating you around this weekend. You ready for dinner? Keep messin' around and we'll skip straight to dessert."

"No, we're going to dinner. We still got later for all of that," I licked my lips and switched towards the door.

He grabbed his wallet off the counter and slid it in his back pocket, while following me out the door. We locked hands and walked towards the elevator for dinner.

The limo pulled up in front an Italian restaurant on the strip. The line was wrapped around the corner. You would have mistaken it for a club and not an eatery. Hakeem said it was so exclusive that they had people on a waiting list from six months to a year. Now, I loved food like the next person, but my ass wasn't about to be waiting for six months to eat at a place. The door was held opened and we stepped out. His hand was on my lower back, guiding me into the restaurant.

"Welcome, Hakeem… I got your table back here," the chef came out and greeted us. First name basis? Hakeem greeted the man and followed him to the back where there were champagne and different types of fruits.

"Thanks man, I appreciate you doing this in a short amount of time."

"Anything; we'll have your food coming out shortly, enjoy."

Hakeem held my chair out and pushed it in for me. To be honest, I had never been on a date like this. Fancy dinner, mannered man and being catered to like this. It felt really nice, and made me see my relationship with Johnathan as a complete failure.

"This is so beautiful, baby… You know just how to make a smile appear on my face," I said, feeling all warm and tingly inside.

He popped the champagne and poured it in my glass, and topped it with a raspberry. "Anything to see a smile on your beautiful face, ma."

Damn, he was making me blush like a little school girl. "You must know some people high up?" I sipped my drink and inquired.

"Nah, I own part of this restaurant," he revealed, and I spit my champagne out.

"You what?"

"A year ago, Antonio graduated culinary school and came to me about opening this restaurant. He needed someone to invest and become partners with him. We grew up on the block together. He moved to Vegas with his pops when we were in high school, but we still kept in touch."

"Wow, so you weren't hesitant about investing in your friend? Even with the possibility of failure? I know the rent on this place is outrageous, it's right on the strip."

"With everything we do there is failure. My mans came to me and had a vision and needed money for the vision. He said he was gonna make us bread, and he has done that. I was bringing in money being Zane's manager, so why wouldn't I help him?"

"You're a good man, Hakeem. He's lucky to have a friend like you." I rubbed his hands, and refilled my champagne glass.

"Thanks baby. I've always been one to move in silence and let my actions speak louder for me. My goal is to get us that big ass house, and please believe I have the bread for it. However, I'm not gonna be house poor. When I buy that house, I want to have bread to continue to live lavishly."

"I am fine with the condo and I love your drive, but I think it's time for me to contribute too." I decided to bring up the meeting I had with Matt. He had called me the day before to meet up next week.

"Oh yeah? What you want to do, Monett?" He raised his eyebrows and accepted the bottle of Jack Daniels.

"Monett knows a photographer that is interested in doing a photo shoot with me. He says he can get me into some good magazines and jumpstart my modeling career."

"Baby, you too damn short to be a model… Fuck you talking about?"

I sighed and rolled my eyes. He knew exactly what I was talking about, but wanted to hear it come out my mouth. "Not runway modeling; covers and stuff. Moet doesn't want to to do it, and I think I can do this."

Taking a shot of his Jack, he poured another before he replied. "Ma, you just had a seed… You don't need to be worrying about that."

Slamming my hand on the table, I looked at him sternly. "No! If you feel one day you're not feeling us, you can just throw us out. We're not married, I don't have rights to your stuff. I need to do this so me and my son will be straight. My ex did everything. I didn't work and you see where I ended up; right at my parents' house."

I promised myself I wouldn't end up like before. I wanted to do something and have money in the bank. Moet finished high school and then went to college to become a nurse. If she and Zane didn't work out, she had a back-up plan. Me on the other hand, had a high school diploma with no skills, or work experience. I did baby sitting for a few friends, but other than that, I didn't have any skills. This modeling thing could take off and I could be making some money, while being pretty.

"Babe, I wouldn't do you like that and you know that. Everything in that condo is yours, so I need to protect myself. When people are mad, their tunes change and I want to make sure I'm good."

"Monett, you're serious right now? Let's not ruin a perfect night, ight?"

I nodded my head and looked up just as the food came out. I had stuffed shells with calamari. Hakeem had penne vodka with a stuffed chicken cutlet. I poked around my food only taking a few bites. I wasn't that hungry.

"If you want to do this modeling thing, then do it. Who am to tell you no. Just know that crib is yours too."

I looked up at him and smiled. He got up and poked his lips out for a kiss, and I gave him one. "Thank you, baby," I cooed, and wiped my lipstick off his lips. He sat back down and we finished eating dinner, while flirting with each other.

*

Hakeem got an urgent call and left dinner early to go handle it. He made sure I got into the limo before he left. He promised to make it up to me. I wasn't angry because I knew he had business to handle. I sat in the back of the limo with my legs crossed, and debated if I wanted to bother Moet again. Throwing caution in the wind, I decided to call. Shit, that was my baby and I needed to know how he was doing.

"Uhh hmmmm, hello?" she moaned into the phone, and I pulled the phone from my ear to look at the screen.

"Moet? What the hell?" I yelled, wondering what the fuck she was doing. Scratch that, I knew what she doing. Where the hell was my son while she was being a porn star?

"Hmmm… what's up, Monett?" she tried to speak, but I guess Zane was handling his business.

"Where the hell is Nauti, while you're being a freak?"

"Mama wanted to keep him overnight. He's sleeping, shouldn't you be… uhhh uh huh, I promiseeeee," she moaned in my ear and I hung up the phone.

I dialed my parents' house and waited for them to answer. My father's voice came through the phone and I smiled. "Hey Daddy, what are you doing?"

"Sleeping, Monett… what else would I be doing at two in the damn morning?" I looked at my phone and laughed. I forgot I was a couple hours behind.

"Sorry Daddy, I was calling to check on my baby boy. How is he?"

He sighed into the phone and woke my mother up. "Here's your mother… I got damn work in the morning. You girls act like the world revolves around y'all asses," he laughed, and I giggled.

"Love you, Daddy. And that's because it does. You spoil us so deal with it."

"Thank God I got me a grandson, and not a granddaughter. Tired of all you women. Love you, Monett." He handed the phone over to my mother, who was yawning into the phone.

"Monett, Nautica is fine; you need to stop worrying like I didn't raise two damn babies myself. He's sleeping and if he wakes up, I'm gonna slap the honey out of you when I see you."

"Honey? Mama, I don't have no honey in me."

"I know; that's how hard I'm gonna slap you that some will come oozing out. Good night, baby… See you tomorrow." She ended the call before I could even get a word in.

Moet's nasty ass was getting her some dick, so I couldn't talk to her. It almost felt like before I had Nauti. Alone all the time, and just left with my thoughts. Tammy crossed my mind, but I knew she would have a big ass fit if I called her this late.

We arrived back at the hotel, and I made my way back to our suite. I opened the door and the lights were low with candles, rose petals and incense lit. The candles created a glow throughout the suite. I followed the rose petals into the bedroom, where Hakeem was standing there with a pair of silky red boxers. His body was all oiled and toned. I bit down on my lip as my panties got super wet.

"You didn't think I would invite you to Vegas to dip for work, did you?" he smirked, and walked closer to me.

He lifted my chin and looked down into my eyes. He placed his lips on mine and rubbed my ass. Zipping down my dress, he pulled down one sleeve and then the other. My dress was now at my waist, and my black lace bra was on display. "Honey Love" by R Kelly was playing on the surround sound. He unbuttoned my bra and let my breasts fall from the cups. In one swift movement, he hiked me up and carried me to the bed, where he took my heels off and kissed my feet. He kissed from my feet to my inner thigh. His cool lips brushing against my warm skin was enough to form goose bumps on my skin.

"I swear I've never met anyone like you, Monett. Each morning when I wake up, I love to see you lying next to me with Nauti on your chest. When you're in the house with a dirty t-shirt and a screaming Nauti, I love you even more. I know what you've gone through and I see you as a strong woman and mother. You did what you had to do for you and your son. Each day, I love you more, and I get excited thinking of this future we're paving," he said in between each kisses he placed on my lips. "I want you to be my wife someday… You hear me?"

My punk ass had tears in my eyes, as he expressed his feelings for me. "I hear you, baby. Every night when you wrap your arms around me, I feel so safe. I feel like everything I've been through was to get to this moment. If it meant going through what I did again, just to get this, I would." I touched his cheeks, and kissed him. The tears won their battle, and they fell down my cheeks.

He kissed me one more time before he pulled the rest of my dress off along with my panties. I opened my legs wide, and dipped my finger into my wet canal. He licked his lips and pulled his boxers down. His long dick was standing at attention; all ten inches of it. I was about to give myself a damn cold sore with the amount of times I licked my lips staring at it.

He dove down and stuck his tongue right into me, while inserting his finger. My mouth was curved in O, and I was moving my hips. I couldn't moan, speak or sign what I was feeling; I was just feeling it. I was moving my hips and getting in the zone, and I felt him flip me over and lick front to back. This nigga was eating my booty like it was his last meal. With Johnathan, we only did missionary and never did oral sex. I found it funny when I used to try and suck him off, how he pushed me away. Should have known that nigga had issues.

He was spreading my legs so damn far and licking me so hard, fingering the shit out of me. I was holding on to my juices, but I let them shits go and I squirted all over his face. "Daddy made you squirt." He flicked his tongue over my pearl and I almost lost my mind.

He lifted my ass up and slipped right into me. He was hunched over me in my ear, and rubbing my breasts. He was nibbling on my ear, as he stroked my pussy with that big shit. This nigga knew how to use his shit, and I was trying to keep up with him. I started twerking my pussy on him and trying to break him, but he took his hands, wrapped them around my hips, and slammed my ass right onto his dick – hard.

"Don't try and outdo daddy, you hear me?" he barked in my ear. When I tell you I was so horny and wet from that shit… However, he knew I did what I wanted. I continued to twerk my ass on him and squeeze my muscles. "Oh, I see you don't listen, huh?"

He pulled it out of me and when I say I gasped when he did, I gasped like I was startled. He was damn near in my liver with that shit. He tooted my ass back up and I was anticipating him to ram that shit into me, but he slapped my ass so hard it started to sting. Under normal circumstances that shit would have hurt like hell, yet this shit felt good. I bent over and twerked my ass while he slapped my shit.

"Look at that big shit shaking," he moaned, and slapped it again. "Get up and come here."

I jumped off the bed, and he made me stand in the middle of the floor, holding my ankles. He bent down and licked my pussy, while telling me if I let go of my ankles he was gonna punish me. Hakeem Stevenson was a fuckin' freak! He flicked that warm tongue on my pussy, as I tried to hold my ankles and prevent myself from falling. His hands spread my ass cheeks apart, and he rammed himself inside of me and I almost collapsed on the floor. I had tears in my eyes because this shit was feeling so good.

"Baby, don't you understand I wanna be your nasty man, I wanna make your body scream, and you will know just what I mean." "Freak Me" came through the speakers and he lifted me up. I wrapped my legs around his waist, and he guided his dick right inside me. I didn't wait for him to take control. I sucked on his neck, and bounced myself right on him. I slid up and down on him, while making him moan. He had to lean on the dresser to keep us from falling. I was squeezing my muscles.

"You like that, baby, huh?" I moaned, while kissing his neck. I kept sliding because this nigga was oiled down.

"Shiiit, yeah, fuck this dick, come on, do it," he demanded and slapped my ass, as he held onto the wall.

We continued like this for two hours, and neither one of us was tired. My body was sore and I was about to tap out. I slammed myself down on his dick one more time, before everything started pouring from me. I felt his warmness come into me, and he walked us over to the bed where we collapsed.

"Damn, that was damn sure worth the wait," he sighed, and pulled me into his arms.

"It was… Thank you for this weekend baby, I really needed this." I kissed him on the lips and laid on his chest. We were both laid out sleeping and naked as the day we were born.

Moet

Thanksgiving was finally here, and I was excited to bust down some food. Big Mama had been here for two days and she was running the house. I couldn't even get my daily dose of dick because she kept knocking on the door. Plus, I didn't want to have sex with Zyair when she was in the house. That didn't stop him from trying to get some pussy from every damn nook in the house. He wanted some sex bad, and I did too. Still, I wasn't fucking with his grandmother under the same roof. Don't get me wrong, the penthouse was massive and she wouldn't even hear us, I just felt weird about the situation. All week I had been running from different grocery stores trying to get everything that Big Mama wanted and needed. I was exhausted and needed that few extra minutes in bed. Zyair had gotten up and gone to the gym so he could feel better about eating for Thanksgiving.

I heard the door open and shut my eyes quickly. Big Mama was on my last nerve about dinner. I didn't think when Zyair said we were doing it at our place that her ass was gonna drag me into everything.

"Moet, wake up! I need you to run down to whole foods and get that drink that Zyair drinks. He's insisted on no soda for him, and needs that," she demanded. I could almost picture her standing by the door with her hand on her hip and a pursed lip.

"Can I just have a quick hour to myself, please?" I groaned and pulled the covers over my head.

"No, you want to be his wife, so you need to go get that boy's stuff. Oh, and stop by a regular supermarket and get some smoked turkey wings. I knew I was missing something. Chop, chop," she said, as she walked out the door.

I swung my legs out the bed and went to the bathroom. After pressing the button on the wall, the floors started to heat as I got ready. Since I was doing errands, I decided to go with a pair of sweatpants, sweat shirt and leather Balmain jacket. I put on a pair of high top Ricardo Tisci Nike Air Force Ones. I pulled my hair into a high ponytail, and put my sunglasses on. When I walked towards the door, Big Mama was on the phone with someone. I just hurried out the door before she asked me to do anything else.

As I was getting in my Range Rover at whole foods, I decided to call Tammy and Monett on three way. “Happy turkey day,” I exclaimed, and they both groaned.

“Moet, I ought to smack the shit out of you… You know what time it is?” Tammy snapped, and I could picture her face.

“Moe, you know I barely get any sleep between working out and Nauti, what you want?”

“Nah bitch, between Hakeem piping that and Nauti,” I cracked a joke, and she giggled like a little school bitch.

“Oh shit, so Keem finally hit that? Oh, that’s why y’all went away for the weekend. How was it?”

When she finally stopped cackling like a damn hyena, she answered, “He’s a freak; that man be having my little ass in all kind of positions, dressing up and doing crazy shit… I ain’t never been fucked like this before, y’all.”

“Hmm, I could remember when Rick used to put it down like that. My baby still gets it right, but mannn, when he used to lift my ass up and sla-”

“Okay, we don’t need your walk down whore lane,” I interjected, and we all laughed.

“Don’t hate, Moe. Wasn’t you answering your phone while moaning to the high gods?” Monett brought up, and I blushed.

“Listen, we ain’t talking about me… What time y’all coming over?” I switched subjects. I remember the night clearly and that shit had been crawling the walls, so of course I wasn’t able to speak.

“Uh hmm, now you wanna switch subjects. I’m coming right on time for dinner… Big Mama done been at my house every day this week. Love my sweet grandmother, but her ass needs to leave me alone," Tammy replied.

"I'm coming around dinner, too. Hakeem's mother has a layover in New York for a couple hours, so we're gonna do a Thanksgiving lunch with her. Plus, it's my first time meeting her. You think you can watch Nauti? I don't wanna bring him around too many people."

"I'm out now, do you want me to pick him up?"

"Oh yass, I knew you were my favorite," she laughed.

"Hoes, I'm going back to sleep. Dion's ass been doing the most since she started crawling. She in all my shit and if she knows better, her ass better stop. She ain't too young for an ass whipping."

"Leave my God baby alone… I'm bout to come get her too," I joked.

"Uh, come on then bitch. You know damn well Nauti is a handful, so leave my baby right on here."

"Umm, alright, get in and I'm coming," we heard Monett moan, and I was the first to start laughing.

"No this hot twat bitch ain't arranging sexcapades while on the phone with us," Tammy blurted, and I laughed so hard I had tears coming out.

"I gotta go y'all; Moe, call me when you're on your way." She ended the call before either of us could answer.

"Hmmm, she done made me wanna wake up Rick's ass. Let me take my hot ass back to sleep. I'll see you later, alright?"

"Later, Tam… Love you."

"Love you too, cupcake."

I continued doing errands and getting stuff that Big Mama kept adding on the the list. I decided to stop by Zyair's gym to see him. I could already tell it was his gym since the paparazzi were camped out in front. I parked in the parking lot and got through the crowd. The whole gym was shut down, and only Zyair, his trainer and the employees were in there. He was running on the treadmill when I walked in.

"Hey baby," I yelled, since it was so loud.

He looked over and smiled. He pressed the button to slow down, and then hopped off. "My baby came to see me. What you doing out so early?"

I screwed up my face at him and he laughed. "You know exactly why I am up this early. Big Mama is driving me crazy. How much longer do you have?"

"I told her to let you sleep in some… she still woke you up early?" he chuckled, wiping the sweat from his face.

"Did she? Hell yeah, and I am so tired."

He grabbed my hand and pulled me to the locker room. "You can drive us home since I got car service. Let me shower and get dressed." He went into his locker and then stopped mid gesture.

He turned back around and rushed to me and pulled down my sweatpants. He lifted me up and put me on the sink. My ass was cold from the cold ass porcelain, but we were definitely about to heat it up. All that could be heard throughout the locker room was our kissing and him slapping my ass. I didn't even care if anyone heard us, I needed to feel him inside of me. I rubbed my hand down his face. My baby was growing this beard, and I was so in love with it. He pulled my sneakers and pants off, and slid my thong to the side before sliding inside of me.

"Uh hmmm," I moaned, as he stuck his penis right inside of me. It fit perfectly inside of me, as he delivered strokes to me that had me screaming. I don't know if it was the fact that we were fucking in a public place or that the dick was good. Shit, I would say both.

"You like that, Peanut? This good right?" he said in my ear as he kissed me on the neck. I was scratching his back and squeezing my muscles.

"Yes, baby I love it, I love it," I moaned, and wrapped my arms around his neck. I was coming and it was gonna be hard. I held him as I unleashed my self onto his dick. He slapped my ass and continued to fuck the shit out of me, as I moaned loudly. I couldn't control it, because he delivered bomb dick each time we fucked. When he tightly gripped my ass, I felt his warmness coat my insides.

"Damn, baby… Shit is always good." He kissed me on the lips, and helped me down. He undressed me and we showered together. He gave me some of his workout clothes and placed my clothes in his gym bag, before we left and headed to pick up Nauti.

*

"Damn, this shit lookin' real good, Big Mama," Zyair complimented and kissed his grandmother.

She hugged him and looked at me. I had to take a nap after that fucking her grandson gave me. Plus, Nauti was colicky and was screaming his head off. So when I finally got a minute to get some sleep, I took that shit. I didn't expect to sleep until dinner, but hell, I needed it.

"No help to you, Moet," she teased me and hugged me. "Now you're on clean-up duty."

"I'll have house cleaning handle that… We're leaving for Miami tonight," he revealed, and I looked at him shocked.

"Miami?"

He turned and looked at me and responded. "I got a small fight I'm doing for charity, so I figured we could use the getaway."

I jumped up and down, excited to be going to Miami. The fact that I could feel the sun on my body made me want to forget dinner and leave. That thought was swept away when the elevator chimed and Monett and Hakeem stepped off.

"Where is my baby boy?" she asked as soon as she saw me.

"He's in his nursery."

"Y'all got him a nursery?" she asked me shocked.

"Umm, he's my nephew and needs a room when he spends time with auntie."

"He 'bout to be booted when our baby come, ain't that right baby?" He rubbed my ass, and kissed me on the forehead.

I saw the look Big Mama gave him, and I knew a conversation between the two of them were soon to happen. Yeah, she liked me, but that was her grandson and she would always be leery of anything.

"Come on, girl," I held Monett's hand, and walked her to where Nauti was. He was asleep in the middle of the customized crib, peacefully.

"I'm gonna leave him for now, but what's up with his grandmother?" she asked as we walked to my room. I still had to finish putting my make up and stuff on.

Monett had never actually fully been in our room. When she did her dramatic running away a month ago, she stayed in the guestroom. "Damn, this room is huge and look at that damn bathroom."

"Check out the closet… He's always spoiling me." She opened the double door and squealed.

"Look at these Chanel bags, and heels… Let me borrow one… wait, let me get this Celine," she called out every time she spotted something different. Zyair had taken me shopping a couple weeks ago and dropped a whole bunch of money on a new wardrobe; on top of the stylist that kept dropping stuff off, my closet was now overfilled.

"Go ahead and take whatever," I told her nonchalantly. I was blessed, and could easily get another one. It was nothing to give back to my family. "Tonight we're flying to Miami," I revealed, and she came out with a pair of Gucci shades on, Celine bag on her arm, and Chanel bag across her chest.

"Damn, Moe. You living the life for real… Shit, I wish I could be that spontaneous."

"You got your little baby now, but I think Hakeem is going too."

She looked at me and then left the room. She quickly came back with a smile on her face. "Mama is going to watch Nauti and I'm coming too!" she squealed.

"Yasss! Mommy and Daddy here?"

"Yep, they just came. She was gonna ask for Nauti anyway."

"I'm really excited. Did you ever think this is where we would be? Like damn, every morning I wake up I have to slap myself."

"It was on my vision board to have a stable family, health and some wealth. Two out of three ain't bad," she joked.

"Quit playing, let's go out there before they think we're antisocial."

We walked back into the kitchen and everyone was quiet. Tammy's mother was sitting at the kitchen counter, and Big Mama was trying to act nonchalant, while my baby had a grill fixed upon his face. Hakeem was sitting on the couch with my parents.

"Hey, how are you?" I spoke, not wanting to get too close. Since nobody was gonna say it, I decided to address it. "Y'all do know Tammy is on her way, right?"

"Big Mama, you should have asked before doing this shit. When you brought it up again last week I changed my mind and said to chill and not do it. Let that shit happen organically and you said alright. Now, she's here!" Zyair barked, and she dropped her spoon.

"Now, I know you're mad, but you better watch that mouth. I don't care how many people you knocked out. Do you hear me? Ms. Little Moet, mind your business and get your self in here and set the dining table," she barked orders, and I slowly grabbed the table settings.

"Aunt Tonya, I appreciate you for getting clean, but a nigga lost a lot of money. I ain't worried about the money, it's the trust. My heart and loyalty is to my cousin, and if she ain't feeling this, I definitely ain't feeling it. Big Mama, sorry for disrespecting you. I'm out," he said, and kissed me on the forehead then headed out with Hakeem.

Big Mama continued to stir the banana pudding like nothing happened, or the fact that my baby didn't just leave. "Dinner must go on anyway. Tonya, go help Moet set the table. She and Zyair is about to get married soon, so y'all need to get to know one another."

I had met Tonya a couple years ago on a street with Tammy. Her ass came out an ally, and I almost knocked her ass out. Tammy cursed her out, and told her not to address her as anything other than a stranger.

"Congrats, I can't wait to see the wedding. I used to do help do all of Tammy's birthday parties," she spoke, and I nodded.

"Okay, I'm sorry. Tammy is my best friend and if she doesn't know about this, I can't support it. Sorry Big Ma-"

The elevator chimed and Tammy and Rick walked into the apartment. I heard her loud mouth from the elevator. She was turned up and I could tell she was happy to be sharing another holiday with Rick.

"Hey Mommy and Daddy," she greeted my parents. "Monett, every time I see your ass you get skinnier and skinnier. How did that meeting go?"

"He had an emergency, but we're meeting really soon."

"Good, you need to show that off… where is your big head sister?" I heard her heels clack, and I tried to duck away from Tonya.

Big Mama didn't look the least bit bothered by the fact that her granddaughter didn't want anything to do with her mother, and her mother was sitting right here.

"Hey, Moe…Oh, hell naw, I'm out. Come on, baby," she walked back out the kitchen and went to get Rick and Dion.

"Tamala, you need to speak to your mother. How long are you going to hold this damn grudge?" Big Mama put her hands on her hips and raised her voice.

"How ever long I want to. No disrespect Big Mama, but I am a grown ass woman. When I say I don't want something, I mean that shit. What you thought, by me seeing her I would change my mind?"

"Tammy, I just want to be here now; I want to know you better and your little family." Tonya's ass just had to speak.

That was like the straw that broke the camel's back, because Tammy spun in her direction with a glare so mean, it made me get chills. "Tonya, you have never been a mother to me. When you got cleaned for a month, you were back on that shit the following month. I went days without eating until Big Mama came and got me. Do you know how it felt to be raised with your cousin who lost his parents, and you have a mother down the street in a trap house? As far as I am concerned, you will never know my children. Yes, Big Mama, I am carrying another child!" she yelled and turned on her heels. I followed her to the front, where she was putting Dion's snowsuit back on.

"Hey Ricky, how you feeling?" I hugged him, and he kissed me on the forehead.

"Hungry as shit," he joked. He had lost a lot of weight, but the fact that he was standing with a cane spoke volumes.

"Tammy, I'll make her leave, can you please stay?" I begged, and she looked at me.

"I'm sorry, Moe. I don't want to be around either of them. I'm going through so much and she knows that, and then she adds more confusion and issues into my path. I'm cool on Big Mama right now." She hugged me. "Where's my cousin?"

"He wasn't with it and left. I'll bring y'all food over before we leave for Miami, okay?"

"Thank you, baby boo." She kissed me and they headed back out.

Thanksgiving was a disaster and I didn't even know where my man went. "Moet, this is some family issues, and we still have to go to your auntie's house. I'll call you later," my mother said, trying to be all nice about bailing on my dinner.

"Later Mommy… Love you guys," I hugged them, and Monett kissed Nauti, who was bundled up and ready to spend time with his grandparents.

"We love y'all too… Thank you again." My mother hugged Big Mama and they promised to call each other to catch up on what just happened.

"Nice meeting you." My mother even hugged Tonya, and I sighed.

After they left, I plopped on the couch with my legs slung over the arms. So much for having a nice Thanksgiving dinner. Shit was a straight disaster, and it was getting me upset just thinking about it. I was waiting for Tonya to leave, but her ass didn't get the hint.

My heart: Take car service to the airplane hanger… You and Monett can get clothes in Miami

Me: Okay, coming. You alright?

My heart: Long as you with me, I'm straight.

I hopped off the couch so fast that I almost caught whiplash. Monett looked up from her phone confused, and Big Mama and Tonya stopped their conversation to look at me.

"We gotta go, Monett," I said, trying to hold my excitement.

"Where you going? We need to eat dinner. Call that grandson of mine and tell him to bring himself here."

"We're leaving for Miami… He has business to handle. See you later, Big Mama," I told her, and kissed her cheek. I grabbed my bag and we left out. I couldn't wait to hit Miami and spend time with my baby. This Thanksgiving was a disaster, and I was ready to forget all about it. We finally got over the prenup thing, and now things were going good.

Zane

We landed in Miami last night and came straight to the hotel. I had a few things lined up for Moet, and she didn't even know it. After handling the legal issues, it was time for us to take that step down the aisle. I know y'all thinking we're gonna get married in Miami, but nah, I wouldn't take her chance to plan her wedding away from her. She was so excited to film this show and plan the wedding of her dreams, so I wouldn't be shit if I took that from her. The sun came through the floor-to-ceiling windows and damn near blinded a nigga. I still hadn't had a chance to speak to Big Mama. I was upset with her for continuing to pursue the issue when Tammy told her that she didn't want to have a relationship with her mother.

Auntie Tonya had done some fucked up shit that made Tammy the way she is. So, I understood why Tammy didn't want to be bothered. Yet, Big Mama crossed the line bringing her in my house for Thanksgiving without at least consulting me about it. She put myself, fiancée and her family in an awkward position. I had my security keeping an eye on her, and she was on her way back to Los Angeles anyway. I'd probably fly in for Christmas Eve and spend time with her. From what security told me, she and my Aunt Tonya both flew back to Los Angles. I guess Big Mama called herself trying to save her daughter. I learned a long time ago that you couldn't save someone that didn't want to be saved.

"I love you so much, baby." Moet wrapped her arms and legs around my back, as I sat on the edge of the bed. She pecked at my neck, and rubbed my chest.

"I love you too, Peanut. What you doing today?" I questioned, and I felt her shrug her shoulders.

I was glad that Monett and Hakeem flew in with us. I had a lot of work to get done and appearances I had to make, and commercials I had to film. I didn't want Moet to get bored, waiting around for me. I also knew I had to warn her about Cabrina being out here. She hadn't been a topic of discussion in the house for a while, and I wanted to keep it like that. Still, I knew Moet's ass got crazy and she would pop off if she had to. The network for her reality show was one of the sponsors of the event. Of course, they had the whole cast interviewing people on the red carpet.

"I don't know, I wanted to spend some time with you, but I know you're busy," she pouted, and I reached up and pulled her into my lap.

"You know daddy got to make the bread. I'll be done by this afternoon; I want to show you something."

"I guess I better go shopping and get something to wear for tonight and today."

"Nah, just call the stylist; she knows your sizes, but give her Monett's and she'll bring some stuff over."

She kissed me on the lips, and wrapped her legs around my waist. "Hmm, where did you come from?" She pushed me down on the bed, and started to take her bra off, but the doorbell rang. "Ugh, who is that?" She climbed off me, grabbed a hotel robe and went to answer the door.

Whoever it was had better been important, because my dick was hard as fuck and my fiancée was about to take care of that for me. She opened the door, and Hakeem and Monett walked through.

"What the hell do y'all want? I'm trying to spend time with my man," Moet snapped and Hakeem laughed, taking his shades off.

"Interrupting something, huh? Your fiancé is a wanted man and needs to start his morning meeting with the hospital that he's fighting for."

"Where did you get new clothes from?" Moet observed her sister's clothes.

Hugging Hakeem's arm, Monett smiled. "My baby took me shopping this morning," she gloated.

"Alright, give us a minute and I'll be ready," I told Hakeem, and he and Monett left.

After I closed the door, I grabbed a squealing Moet and ran into the room. I threw her on the bed and handled my business. I ate that pussy until she squirted right into my mouth, then I slammed that tight and juicy pussy right on top of me, and she rode the shit out of me until we both came. We could have gone hours, but I had to get going. She collapsed beside me and closed her eyes. I just knew she was going to go sleep, and she did in four seconds flat. I showered and got dressed for the day. I always had luggage packed on my jet. Now, I had to tell Moet to do the same thing.

"I'll see you later, baby. The stylist will be over here in an hour, so make sure you let her in." I said, watching her with her legs spread open and knocked out.

"Uh mmmm," she groaned, and I kissed her and slipped my fingers inside her wetness. I licked my fingers; I loved the taste of my personal Moet.

After doing all my shit for the charity, I was free until tonight. I had called up to the room and told Moet to meet me in front of the hotel. After convincing her greedy ass that I would buy her something to eat, she finally came downstairs. I had to do a double take because my baby was looking good enough to eat, but hot enough not to touch. She had cut-up booty shorts on with a jean button-up shirt tucked in. Her pretty ass toes were in a pair of black strappy heels, and a black Celine sat right up on her arm. I knew that shit cost me a grip, but her ass was looking too damn good.

"Damn ma, you looking good... look at that cake sitting all high in them shorts." I tapped it and she giggled and kissed me.

"You know I try, boo… what the heck is this?" She pointed to the Poloris sling shot I bought this morning. I saw my nigga Safaree on one a couple weeks back, and went to go cop one myself.

"Just something to cruise the streets of Miami with. Get in baby," I said, and helped her inside.

I had my baby out in a sling shot cruising the Miami blocks. I had my nigga Tory Lanez "Say It" blaring, and I was whipping this shit with one hand. Everybody was in town for this celebrity charity event. I wanted to show my baby the town real quick, and what better way to do it in a two seat Polaris sling shit. Moet was in awe, as her hair blew in the wind and we cruised.

"Love how you spin around on it," she sang, and winked at me.

"You gonna do that tonight?" I shifted my dick in my pants.

"Only if you want me to," she licked her lips.

Now when I tell you my baby was a certified freak, I ain't even gonna disclose to y'all half the shit we be on, but just know she does this shit better than any of these chicks out here. We pulled into a gated community, and she looked confused. We cruised the block until we came across a nice ass modern house with a waterfall and shit in it. She was so busy looking at me for answers, she didn't even notice her sister across the street.

"Peanut, go on and look around our new Miami crib," I nonchalantly said, and she screamed.

"We're moving? Baby, we're moving?"

"Nah, nah, but we need a house in Miami so we can get away sometime," I explained, and she kissed me on the lips and jumped out.

"Monett? What are…Yesss, that's your house?" Both sisters jumped up and down while me and Hakeem leaned on his car.

Me and Hakeem had been planning on copping real estate in Miami for a minute, so when this deal turned up, we couldn't do anything but take it. I didn't visit Miami often, but now I had a reason to be out here often. Shit, with the winter coming, I was damn sure about to be down here. That was the reason I moved from New York to California in the first place. I opened the garage and there sat two twin Bentleys for us while we stayed in Miami.

"Zyair, you need to take this back, it's too much," Moet said, hugging me.

She had tears in her eyes and kept staring at me like she was waiting for me to say sike. "Ma, stop stressing about this. I know your parents are gonna wanna spend some time here when pops retire. This shit got a golf course on it."

I wasn't lying, our backyard was a golf course. I knew Richard was gonna have a hell of a time relaxing here. "Well baby, I need to show you something in our new house," Monett cooed, and took Hakeem.

That nigga was smirking like he had the best kept secret. In all honestly, the Rubbin girls weren't shit to mess with. They were respectful, had morals and freaks; let me not forget beautiful and had nice ass bodies.

We walked into the house and it was the shit. Glass staircases, with walls that had water running down them. The scheme was black and grey. The infinity pool ran right into the golf course, of course with a protective glass on it. Moet couldn't keep her hands off me as she walked around the house. I planned to get furniture and shit and have her do what she wanted, but for now, we got the house and that's all I needed.

"I mean, this sink is really nice," Moet said, as she unbuckled her shorts and dropped them to the floor. Still in her heels, she stepped out the shorts. She jumped on the sink and opened her legs wide enough for me to see her squeaky pink pussy.

"You want to bring this in right, huh?" I stroked my dick and got ready to dig up in that shit again. We were bringing the house in the right way.

*

After fucking on the sink, shower, window and even doing it in the pool, we had to get ready for tonight. Our stylist had everything together soon as we stepped through the door. Now, we were stepping on the red carpet looking like nothing but money. Our colors were black and gold. Monett and Hakeem were right behind us, as we walked the carpet and took pictures. Moet was so smitten with me, that she was kissing me and taking cute ass photos. Usually I just grilled the pictures and kept it pushing.

Now we had to be interviewed, which I wish I didn't have to do. Cabrina came over to us with her microphone and I sighed. She would be the one to rush over to us with her petty ass.

"Zane and Moet, how are you guys? You have a second?" Hakeem nudged me and I nodded my head. He saw my ass fixing my lips to say something other than yes, so he had to keep me from going off.

"Yeah, what's good?"

"So, you are here fighting One Sept tonight… any animosity between you two?"

"Nah, that's my nigga and we go back since training days. I'm excited to kick it with him."

"Okay, I didn't know that little information… I see you have your fiancée here, what are you wearing, Moet?"

"I'm wearing Balmain, and the heels are Giuseppe. My baby is wearing the same thing," Moet answered, sounding polite.

"Okay, okay, well you're looking nice and plump," Cabrina took a little dig. "Are you expecting?"

Moet's face dropped, and her fist balled, but I watched my baby calm down and come into her own. "Umm, no, I am just naturally thick and love my size. But, I hate to see that a thick woman can't just be thick; it has to assumed that she's expecting."

Cabrina didn't have shit to say, but the camera man kept telling her to go. "Oh, I see you bringing it for the big girls. What can we expect from you now that you're in the limelight?"

"We'll, me and my baby are doing a reality wedding special on our wedding that's coming really soon… I can't release too much, but you'll see it coming soon."

"Okay, well we can't wait to see you do your thing, Zane," she cooed, and touched my shoulder.

"Bet." We walked inside to have a good time before it was time for me to bust some ass.

Chapter Seven

Tammy

"Stop being so hardheaded and stay yo' ass in the room. If you just go to sleep then the noise I'm making in my room wouldn't bother you, now would it?" my mother scolded for the third time that night. She was having another one of her infamous parties and everyone was making so much noise.

My eight-year-old self couldn't sleep if there were any noises, especially a loud speaker, yelling adults and the sound of clinking bottles. When I knocked on my mama's door, her man got irritated and sent her to make sure I stayed in the room. Instead of being comforting and telling me it'll be okay and try and get some sleep, she scolded and tapped me on the ass. Once she closed the door, and I heard her yell "Get it." I rolled over to try and get sleep. It was already three in the morning and I had to be up for school in a couple hours. I laid in bed thinking of my cousin, Zyair. I loved spending time over he and Big Mama's house. There was always food, heat and quiet nights. I was lying in bed starving because the last time I ate was when I had lunch at school, and then an apple for after school.

I turned my head because I heard the door creak. It was my mother's best friend's husband. Every time I saw him, he gave me candy and always called me a pretty girl. He closed the door behind him and sat on the edge of my bed.

"Uncle Black, you gotta get out so I can get some sleep," I muttered, but he didn't budge. I lightly tapped him with my foot, and he looked at me.

He slowly took my blanket off of me, and I tried to pull it back, but he snatched it harder. I was lying in bed with my night gown and slipper socks. "Tamala, you need to just go back to sleep and let Uncle Black check and see if you have something."

"Have something? Uncle Black, I am fine."

My word wasn't good enough, because he pulled my dress up and pulled my panties down, then stuck his finger inside my little vagina. I kicked, screamed and fought, but he was too strong. I felt his nasty ass tongue touch my privates and screamed.

"Yo, what the fuck!" Glenn, my mother's boyfriend yelled, rushing in and knocking him on the floor.

My face was filled with tears and I was trembling. I was so scared, confused and just wanted my mommy to hold me. Glenn commenced to whipping Black's ass so bad that his wife and two other men had to take him to the emergency room. To this day, he was in an old folk's home because he had brain damage.

"Get that nigga out this house!" he yelled and went through my drawers, while mumbling shit. He found me panties, pants, socks and a shirt, and helped a frightened me get dressed. "Tonya! Bring your ass back here girl!" he hollered.

My mother came stumbling in the room giggling, high as a kite. "W... what happened baby?" she slurred.

"Black was just back here touching on her!"

"Oh, she okay?" She leaned on the wall, nodding off.

"Look how scared she is! She's shaking and wet the damn bed!"

"Baby, go take a s...s...hower and then go back to bed," she continued to fall all over the place and slur.

"Nah, when I first found out about this shit, you said it was under control, you were handling this and we would be a family. Two years and you're still on the same shit, if not worse!"

My mother didn't hear his rant because she had nodded out. He didn't bother to wake her, he just packed me some stuff and finished dressing me and we left. We took the bus a couple blocks down to my grandmother's house, where he dropped me off. He never disclosed what happened to my grandmother, and if she knew what happened she wouldn't be so gung hoe on reuniting us together.

Now, Glenn was a good man and I was still in his life. That night probably opened his eyes to a lot of shit and made him change his ways. He joined the army, and was deployed for a couple years overseas. When he came back, he had so much gifts and love for me. I mean the man was in my life for two years. I still had lunch or dinner with him a couple times out the year. He was married now with his own wife and children, but it was something about him; it was like he was my unofficial father.

"Damn baby, I've been calling you for a while now," Rick brought me back to reality, as he saw the tears pouring from my cheeks. Besides Glenn and me, Rick also knew about what happened. I told him about it the first time he went down on me. It took me a while to get used to it, and I finally become comfortable with it. My mother's ass was too high to remember anything, and I didn't feel like reliving it by telling her dumb ass about her poor decisions.

"Oh, I'm sorry. I was thinking about something… What you need?" I wiped my tears, and started washing the dishes again. Moet's ass never did bring the food, but I didn't hold her to it. I had cooked earlier that day anyway, so I didn't need anymore food.

"What's the matter?" Rick hugged me and I sighed. I loved this man with all of me. I don't know what I would do if he wasn't around. He was the only one that could put up with my smart ass mouth, and my smart ass comebacks.

"Nothing, Rick. I don't want to talk about it. What did you need?"

"I was showing your ass the damn Christmas tree you wanted. We putting one up for, Dion?"

Christmas… that was the only thing that made me smile. I loved the holiday season and everything that came with it. It wasn't the fact that you got gifts, cards and other shit. It was something about doing for someone else and making them happy with your thoughtfulness. Y'all know my ass ain't all sappy like this. Yet, Christmas did it to me.

"Oh yeah, we can go this weekend to pick it out. What time is radiation?"

"In a little bit; moms is coming with me." I rolled my eyes and nodded. Zyair had been quiet about the lawsuit because he wanted me and Rick to handle it. They knew they fucked up and wanted to settle. Me, I didn't care about the money, but the lawyer wanted to get what we were suing for, which was a 3.4 million dollars.

"I'm gonna take a quick nap before Dion wakes up. I'm so tired and needs a minute, babe."

"As you should. You gotta stop running around like this, Tam. Take care of yourself too."

"I hear you," I sighed, as I walked upstairs to lay down. Soon as my face hit the pillow, I was knocked out.

I don't know how long I had been out, but I heard someone banging on my damn door. Now, why did everyone want to try me? I rushed downstairs and opened the door. Moet was standing there with wine, *Boston Market* and a gift bag.

"When the hell is your ass going back to work?" I questioned yawning, and she hugged me.

"Is that how I get greeted? Sorry for waking your crabby ass, I forgot my key." She walked past me and went into the kitchen. "I decided to take some time off and enjoy being a fiancée and traveling with my man."

"Ain't that the life, huh?"

"Yeah, he wanted me to cut back and my job pissed me off, so I'm giving their ass a little break. Plus, I don't spend as much time as I want to with you. I wanna help with Dion and give you guys a break once in a while."

"Look at you trying to be a good God mommy. How you know I was starving?"

"You look skinny and need to eat." She turned her face up, but smiled.

"Bitch! Where's big head at?" I asked about my cousin.

"Him and Hakeem are having a boy's night out. Talking about hitting the strip club and shit. Monett is being a mommy, so I want to spend time with my bestie. I know you need some girl time."

"You ain't lying about that. How's the baby fever going?"

She looked at me and laughed. "I hadn't thought about it since me and him talked. Ugh, it was so stressful thinking about that all the damn time. It was crazy to try and get pregnant before getting married. I honestly was tripped out for that," she laughed and placed the plate in front of me. "There's enough in here, Rick wants some?"

"He's having dinner at his mama's house with Dion." I rolled my eyes, and took the plates into the living room. She followed behind me with our wine glasses, and kicked her shoes off.

We were kicked up on the couch laughing and catching up on our shows. It felt so good to laugh and be with my best friend and not think of other things. "Bitch, I thought you poured me a little glass of wine and this shit sparkling cider," I laughed, shoving her.

"I don't need my second baby coming out like duhh." We laughed and I chugged the apple cider.

"What's going on with the wedding special? I saw you mention it on the red carpet with that hoe."

"Girl, I really don't even know if I want to do it anymore. I was doing it to get back at that hoe, but no matter what I do, she'll still try and get with Zyair. At this point, the ball is in his court about it."

"You know he's done with her, right? He's not interested in her ass at all. I think y'all should do a small wedding with just family, and that's it. You don't have to prove your love to anybody, Moet. After you do that big wedding, that hoe will still be a hating hoe."

She nodded her head and sipped her wine. "Zyair really didn't want to do it, but I made him. See, this is why I need more Tammy time," she hugged me and giggled.

"You and me both. So what else y'all did in Miami?" I asked, because I knew she was about to tell me some juicy shit. Right now, I lived through her life.

Her eyes widened and she turned and faced me. "Girl, he brought us a house in Miami. It's huge and really nice. He said he can't do winters in New York, so we'll be spending some time in Miami."

"For real? Well when do me and Rick pack? Wait, what does that mean for your job, Moet?"

"I've been taking some time off. Ever since I was suspended, they pissed me off, so I'm spending time doing shit I actually wanna be doing. After the new year, I plan to return, so I'm good."

"Oh alright, I know you worked hard to get where you are and I don't want to see you throw it away to become just Zane's wife."

"Hell no, you know I love my job. How's Rick?"

I sighed and turned the television off. We weren't even watching the damn show. "He's doing the radiation to see if that shit will shrink. If not, he'll have surgery. I'm hoping that it shrinks."

"Me too, ugh, I miss just hanging under you," she sighed and laid in my lap, as I ran my hand through her hair. This was my sister, my baby and everything. It wasn't too many people that could remain friends after going through all the shit life kept throwing at us.

Rick ended up calling me and telling me he was staying over his mother's house. I didn't bother to argue because that bitch knew what she was doing. Me and Moet climbed into my big bed with food and snacks, while watching Netflix until we fell asleep. Sometime during the night, I heard Zyair come in and wake her up to come home. It was so cute that he couldn't sleep without her. I felt him kiss me on the cheek and cover me back up. I cuddled more into the bed and knocked the hell out; it felt good to get some sleep. Between Dion and Rick, I never could sleep past a certain hour, and I was damn sure about to sleep beyond those hours.

Monett

I was still coming down off my high from Miami. It had been two weeks since Hakeem bought us a beautiful house in Miami, with a pool and everything. I couldn't wait to come home and tell my mama. I knew he had been up to something. Every time I cleaned his office, I noticed he was looking at real estate in Miami. I just thought he was going to buy some to flip, but he actually bought us a second home. I hopped out my BMW truck and pulled Nauti out the back. I swung his diaper bag over my shoulder and locked up my car. I walked up the stairs to my parents' house and opened the door with my key.

"Rich?" my mother called out from the kitchen.

"No, it's me and your fat grandson, Mama!" I yelled back, and she rushed from the kitchen and grabbed the carrier from me.

My mama was in love with her grandbaby. She spoiled his little self and was obsessed with calling and hearing him snore when he slept. "Look at nanny's fat baby boy," she cooed, and took him out his chair. I dropped his bags and followed them into the kitchen.

She was in the kitchen cooking lunch and making some pies. Ugh, I loved her holiday pies, and apparently everyone else within a twenty block radius. She made decent money making these pies for the holiday.

"How you feeling, Mama?" I kissed her cheek, and sat at the kitchen table.

She was in the living room getting Nauti's bouncer out so she could sit him on the island. "I'm good, baby. How are you? I feel like I barely see you and your sister."

"I'm good; we're just so busy. I need to make more time for my favorite girl," I smirked and she smiled.

"That's what your lips say."

"So, I have some news, Mama," I started and she stopped messing with the bouncer.

"You're not pregnant are you?"

"Heck no, no more babies are coming out of me until I have a ring on my finger. Hakeem bought us a house in Miami on a golf course. It's a whole community."

She looked up at me with wide eyes. "You're moving to Miami?" She almost had worry in her eyes.

"No, it's a vacation house. You know, to get away from the cold weather. I want you and Daddy to come stay with us; Zane got Moe one too."

"So they're just buying houses like purses? Now baby, I don't want to be negative, but Moet is marrying Zane. They have a prenup in place that protects both of them. What do you have with Hakeem?"

I sighed and shrugged my shoulders. "His word."

She came around the counter and wrapped her arms around me. "Baby, his word isn't going to protect you and my grandbaby. I'm not saying rush into a marriage, but see about drawing up an agreement where if something happens, you're protected. Make sure you get your name on the leases and deeds."

"I hear you, Mama. I believe him when he says he would never do something like that."

"Hakeem is a good man, but it's about making sure you are taken care of. You see what happened with Johnathan. He owns that house, so you had to leave. Hakeem is no damn Johnathan, but be smart."

"I hear you, Mama. I met his mama on Thanksgiving. She had a layover here, and she's really nice."

"That's nice; when can I meet her?"

I shrugged my shoulders. "Hakeem says she travels a lot, and they don't have the best relationship. It was almost awkward between them, but when he excused himself to take a call, me and her talked and she told me she did a lot of things she's not proud of, and some of those things Hakeem witnessed, which is why their relationship is so strained."

"Hopefully, they can come together and be a family. Hakeem knows he got us too, right?"

"He knows, Mama."

Matt: I'm on my way to the restaurant… see you soon beautiful

Me: I'll be on my way now, boo.

I sent Matt the text message back and got up and kissed my mother. "Mama, I'm going to a meeting, can y-"

"You know you don't even need to ask. My baby will be right here with Nanny baking pies."

"Thank you, Mama," I hugged her and headed out the door. I hopped in my car and sped off. I couldn't wait to have this meeting. Stuff kept getting in the way that prevented us from having it sooner, but now that I was free and Matt was now in New York permanently, we both had time to discuss some stuff. It took me no time to make it to the restaurant. I parked, got out and walked inside. I beat Matt here, so I sat down and pulled my phone out.

Johnathan: can I see my son?

Me: Whenever you are free. You can come to my parents' house in like two hours.

Johnathan: Can I take him for the rest of the week

Me: Lol, no

Johnathan: Umm, he's my son too. I want to spend time with him, Monett!

Me: Negative. If you want to come to my parents' house you can… I'll be there until 4

I looked up and Matt was walking into the restaurant. Johnathan never replied, so I guess he didn't want to see his son that badly.

"Hey pretty girl, how are you?" Matt greeted, giving me a hug and kiss.

"I'm doing better, how are you?" I sat down and we ordered some drinks and appetizers.

"Well, I just got engaged to my honey boo… We've been together for three years and he finally popped the question. You've gotten skinnier since I saw you. Damn that body tight." He slapped hands with me and put some sugar into his sweet tea then stirred it.

"Okay, so now that I got you here... I'm ready to run full force into getting your career off the ground. I don't know if I mentioned it, but I am starting my own modeling agency. Last time I saw you, I was out to lunch with two models I was thinking of welcoming to our team. MEZ modeling agency is very particular with the models we pick, and I want you!" he said with so much excitement.

I put my hand over my mouth and gasped. "Seriously?"

"Girl, yes! I have a few models that I've been working with, but they are runway. You're far too short for that, but you have this body that I can see in magazines and clothing ads. I have this shoot set up for Versace for next weekend, and I need a model and you're perfect. I kept rescheduling because I wanted to come correct before stepping to you. Now, your sister and you on this cover would be dope."

"Moet isn't even interested in modeling."

"Girl, don't I know…you didn't let me finish. I think you can kill this spread alone. Soon as we get the contract signed, I'll send you over the details. Now, I'm the photographer on this shoot, so I'll be there to comfort you and make sure you kill."

"Ugh, I am so excited! Where do I sign?"

"No, baby girl. Take this home, read it over and make sure you're straight. I'm building a business relationship with you, but I also want a friendship with you. Have your lawyer, manager or whoever look it over."

"You are so right… I'll do that, but I appreciate the opportunity."

We continued to have lunch and talk about anything. Matt was hilarious and he literally had me crying the entire time. I had to excuse myself a few times to go to the bathroom. I knew this business deal was going to be the best one. Now, I just needed to have this looked over.

*

"I think you should sign. Everything looks good," Hakeem said, looking over the contract.

"Really, Keem?"

"Yeah baby, everything seems like a go on that. Now you need management, and I was thinking you could sign to Stevenson management." He smirked and handed me back the contract.

"Oh really?"

"I mean… I could refer you to some managers that I know."

"Baby, do you think that'll mess with our relationship?"

"Nah, because I won't let it. Let me make you some bread and then we'll think about having you come to Stevenson Management. I bet I'll change your mind."

"You think so?" I said, and got up and pulled down my jeans. I pulled my legs out and took my thongs off and walked over to his desk. I climbed on his desk and spread my legs right in front of him.

"Damn, you feeding me good tonight." He licked his lips and dived right into my goodies. Sex with Hakeem had been so damn good that we couldn't get enough of each other. Any and everywhere we found a place to fuck, we did. We had just gotten our pass into the mile-high club, when we fucked in the bathroom in Zane's jet.

He didn't waste anytime lapping up my juices and nibbling on my pearl. I had my head thrown back, and was moaning so loud that I was glad that my mom kept Nauti over night. I pushed my goodies right into his face, and he put his hands around my waist and brought me closer. I guess that wasn't enough for him, because he picked me up and threw me on the couch in his office. He took his pants off and shoved himself right into me, as I held onto his neck and we kissed. We were so deep into our lovemaking that we hadn't noticed Moet walking into the office.

"I'm just gonna go ahead and give your key back. I'll knock like everyone else," she said, covering her eyes. We didn't even bother to answer her, because we continued fucking while she said all of that. "Y'all nasty asses could have stopped… I'll call you tomorrow," she called out from the hallway.

That just gave us more reason to go harder, and Hakeem picked me up and sat me on the edge of his desk, as he fucked the shit out me. Damn, I ain't never had dick so good, and the fact that we fucked anywhere and didn't care, made the experience that much better. We continued to fuck in his office for the rest of the night. It was so damn hot, the windows started to fog up. I couldn't help but wonder what Moet wanted, but when Hakeem stuck his tongue in my booty hole, that thought floated away along with all the breath in my body.

Moet

My first stop after coming from Monett and Hakeem's house should have been a damn therapist's office. Here I was coming over to share my news, and her ass was getting her back dug in. The fact that their asses still continued to fuck while I stood there, had me blown. I guess when you're getting dicked down so good, you wanted to share your news. I shook my head, as I got into my truck and pulled off. I had a trunk filled with gifts, since Christmas was coming very soon. I loved this holiday, but I wanted to be shopping with Zyair. He was so busy training and handling the other business deals he had. After the fight in Miami, which he won for charity, he had been working harder it seemed.

Tonight, I was cooking dinner and I planned to talk to him about the wedding. It had been a couple weeks since I talked to Tammy about pulling out from the wedding special. I hadn't shared that with him, and tonight I planned to. I stopped and got everything I needed for tonight and headed home. The doorman helped me upstairs with all my bags, and then I kicked off my shoes to get comfortable. I put on some sweats and tied my hair up and started to cook. I was making some bison burgers with sweet potatoes fries. I wanted to do something nice for him since he had been so busy working.

I knew me choosing not to do the wedding special would make him happy. The network had been calling and emailing me about doing promo shoots for the show. I hadn't told Navi to let them know, but I planned to send that email tonight. A small intimate wedding, with my daddy and Rick walking me down the aisle was what I wanted. I wanted Rick to walk me down the aisle; besides my daddy, he had always been the second man to protect me. When he met Ki, he told me that I should dead it and he wasn't feeling him. Both he and my daddy said the same thing.

Two hours later, and dinner was done. Zyair walked through the door and came and found me. He looked tired as hell, but had a smile on his face once his eyes laid on me. I hugged him and kissed him before showing him the food I cooked.

"Hey baby, you alright?" I asked and kissed him.

"My trainer worked the shit out of me, but I'm cool… What's good with you?"

I smiled and poured him a glass of wine. "I'm fine; I went Christmas shopping and got you something."

"Oh yeah?" he smiled, and I handed him a bag.

He slowly opened the bag and pulled out a long box. I was so excited for him to see my gift. It wasn't much you could get a man that had everything and could buy anything. He opened it and looked at it before his face lit up. "For real, you carrying my baby?"

I squealed and jumped up and down. "Yes, you said if we stopped thinking about it, and look, it happened."

"Come here, Peanut." I went and sat on his lap and he rubbed my stomach, kissing me on the lips. "We're really doing this, huh? 'Bout to be those fly ass cool parents."

"You already know, babe. I'm gonna still be Moet," I popped my gums, and he laughed at me being over the top.

"Damn, come on, I wanna make love to my baby girl," he said, and I shook my head.

"Nope, not until I am out the woods. We can only tell close family, not the world."

He took my hand and placed it on his rock hard dick, and looked up at me with pleading eyes. "You gonna leave him like that?"

"Yep! I also pulled out the wedding special. I think our vows should be secret and not broadcasted to the world."

He looked pleasantly surprised. "What made you decide that?"

"I don't know; I just felt like I needed to get Cabrina's ass back and hurt her with our love. Now I'm seeing I don't need to prove shit to anybody. I'm living in the big houses, got the big ring and carrying your baby. It's so obvious that she's irrelevant and by me stooping to her level, I am giving her life."

"Look at my baby being all mature and using her words," he joked and took a bite from the burger. "So when you wanna take a leap down the aisle?"

"Valentine's Day," I replied, and he looked up and nodded. "A new year and a fresh start. I wanna be married when the baby is born."

"I'm feeling that...The Whitfield's," he laughed. "You already got the cards and anything you need to pay for it."

I kissed him and ran my hand through his little fro he was growing. "Love you, babe."

"You already know I love you, mama." He kissed me, and we continued to eat dinner.

I cleared the dishes before going to shower and getting in bed with a naked ass Zyair. His dick was rock hard and he was winking at me. "Boy, take your butt to bed. Nothing going in here until I am past that stage."

He groaned and kissed me before pulling me into his arms, and we feel asleep.

*

"Now that you found the venue; how many people are you inviting?" Navi asked, as she wrote down some stuff. I decided to have her help me with the wedding. She had been spending time with her family often, and she was ready to get back to work.

"I'm thinking fifty people. I don't want anybody that isn't family or a close friend. I wrote down the list this morning. I'll email it to you when I get home. Now we have the venue, we need food, drinks, music, dresses and tuxes."

"Don't forget wedding bands. Zane, is getting those so you can cross that off the list. I've lined up a make-up and hair stylist already."

"I'm praying my wedding dress is ready by then."

"It will be, since we ordered back when you were doing the show. I'll email him and make sure we're good."

I was having a custom made Givenchy wedding dress with a huge train made. Since we were cutting corners with everything else, I wanted to have this beautiful dress made for pictures. I found a beautiful castle in Long Island where the wedding would be held. The event coordinator even made sure that paparazzi wouldn't be able to fly over and snap pictures. Let me explain something, I have matured and although I wasn't bashing Cabrina's skull in, or doing the wedding special, I was still petty as fuck. Pettiness runs in my blood; believe it or not, my mama was a petty chick. I was still going to release our wedding pictures on the day of her show. Yeah, just call me Petty LaBelle and I'm handing out petty pies.

"Okay, I'm gonna get the girls together to get their dresses done, too."

"Later Moe. My baby is getting out of school soon, and I need to pick her up."

"Okay, thanks again Navi," I said, and hopped in my truck. This was going to be a breeze. I couldn't wait to take a step down the aisle with my baby. I rubbed my stomach and smiled. Things were finally looking up.

Zane

Between wedding planning and working out, along with other shit I had to tend to, I was tired as fuck. Now, add in the fact that your girl didn't want to fuck you and you were horny as fuck! I was horny as fuck and needed some of my personal bottle of Moet, but her ass was fronting. It was Christmas Eve, and Moet had everyone over to the house, while heating up eggnog and handing it out. Big Mama and Auntie Tonya were spending Christmas in Jamaica, and she still wasn't speaking to me. I called to talk to her, but she refused to speak to me. Everything in my life was all right, but I couldn't take my Big Mama not speaking to me.

"I don't know who the hell makes warm egg nog," Tammy complained, but turned the cup up to her mouth and chugged it.

"Your greedy ass drinking it," I said, and she threw a pillow at me. "Babe, was it necessary for all of us to wear matching pajamas? These footsie shits are annoying," I complained, and Rick laughed.

I was glad my nigga was doing better than expected. He was getting out the house more and being around family. He was still skinny as shit and bald, but long as he was laughing and chilling, I was cool.

"Baby, this is part of Christmas." She came out the kitchen holding Nauti, who had the baby version of our pajamas on. Dion was sleeping in the nursery with the same pajamas on too. "Now, we have an announcement to make," she smiled, and I just knew she was going to announce the pregnancy.

"Can I have my eggnog?" Hakeem asked, while Monett nudged him.

"Don't be rude, Keem... What happened, Moe?"

"A nigga thirsty though," he continued, and we laughed.

"She thinks she's the shit since on that new Versace catalog, boom!" Tammy laughed, and Monett did a model walk in front of us."

"I'm pregnant!" Moet blurted, and Monett stopped and looked at her.

"Wahhhhhhhh!" Tammy and Monett screamed together, and bum rushed her into hugs and kisses. Thankfully, I took my little nigga, Nauti, or he would have been in the middle of all of that.

"Yass, we're gonna be pregnant together!" Tammy danced around.

"I'm pregnant too," Monett announced, and Hakeem choked on his eggnog. Rick had to move over and pat that nigga on the back, because he was choking so hard. "I'm joking, Hakeem!" She ran over and patted his back, laughing.

"I'm gonna be a God mother!" Tammy exclaimed with tears in her eyes.

"And I'm gonna be an auntie!" Monett hugged her sister and they added Tammy into their big ass hug.

"Congrats, nigga," Rick said, after making sure Hakeem was done choking. We shared a brotherly hug and then Hakeem got his choking ass up and congratulated me.

"Oh Rick, I wanted you to walk me down the aisle with my daddy," Moet said and hugged him. "You know you are like a big brother to me." She had tears coming down her cheeks.

"Moe, you know I got you." He hugged her and kissed her forehead, while Tammy tried to act like she wasn't crying.

I pulled her in my arms and hugged her tightly. "Stop crying, lemon head."

"I... I got something in my eyes," she lied and I mushed her head.

"Yeah, yeah, stop fronting."

"Shut up, and congratulations. You better call that grandmother of ours and tell her."

"I will."

We continued to celebrate until we all fell asleep. Moet made sure everybody stayed the night over so we could all open gifts in the morning. Of course, I tried to get some booty before bed, but she shut my ass down – again.

I felt like I had just laid down when I felt Moet's thick ass jumping on me. "Babe, it's Christmas!" she yelled, while smothering me with big ass kisses.

"Come on, let me sleep," I complained, and she pulled the covers off of me. My damn toe busted through the footsie, so my big toe was freezing and shit.

"Come on, baby. I wanna open presents and show you what I got you!" she squealed and left the room.

I got up, brushed my teeth and fixed myself before going into the kitchen. I didn't even know her moms and pops came last night, because they had the same pajamas. Tammy was up and smiling, while giving Rick his medicines. Hakeem and Monett were playing with Nauti and smiling. Damn, this felt like family right here.

"Good morning, Son, merry Christmas!" Richard said, and hugged me.

I told Navi what I wanted to get everyone, and she did just that. Some of the gifts were so damn big, I had to drop extra money to make sure everything went through in time.

"What's good, Pops! When y'all get here?"

"Early this morning. We were supposed to here last night, but I fell asleep. Congrats on the baby," he said, and patted my back.

"Thank you, thank you," I said and hugged her mother, who was heading my way full speed.

"I'm gonna be a grandmother for the second time… Congrats baby," she hugged me.

After we ate, we all sat in front of the big ass tree and passed around gifts. Moet got me a Rolex, some pajamas and some colognes. I appreciated it because she bought it with her money.

"Thank you, baby," I kissed her and she laughed, and egged me to try the watch on.

After everyone opened their gifts, me and Hakeem decided to give everyone their gift. I handed Tammy and Rick an envelope, handed Moet an iPad and her parents a thick yellow folder.

"I have an iPad," she said, and I smirked.

"Turn it on and go to the videos." She did as she was told and I watched as her face transformed in front of me. There was a video of our house in Miami, with new furniture and everything. Her closet there was stocked with mad shit. She jumped up and down, but didn't drop that damn iPad.

"Baby, it's beautiful!" she screamed, and showed her parents. Both she and her mother jumped up and down.

"Baby girl, that house is beautiful. I see some green back there, it's a golf course?" Richard said with a smile.

"Pops, you already know I got you… you and moms got y'all own suite in both houses," I said, and cued Hakeem to give Monett her gift.

He handed her an iPad and her eyes lit up before he turned it on. Once she sat there watching it, tears came down her eyes. "It's so nice, Hakeem. It's beautiful," she cried, and he handed her an envelope.

He did their entire house and got her a new Porsche that was sitting right in the driveway. She had tears streaming down her face. She opened the envelope and flew into his arms crying.

"What's in the envelope?" Tammy's nosy ass asked, and we all laughed.

"That house is hers; her name is on the deed and everything," I said, speaking up for them. Hakeem kept laughing and telling her to stop crying.

"That is so sweet, baby," her mother hugged her.

I watched Tammy open her present and she smiled. "Big head, how did you know I wanted to go to Jamaica?"

"I figured you and Rick could use some time. I've hired a nanny so you can spend fam time and then have y'all alone time." I hugged both of them.

"I appreciate that, bruh." Me and Rick dapped.

"Y'all alre-"

"OMG!!!! OMG!!!" Moet's mother screamed and jumped up and down. I smirked because I already knew why she was screaming.

"What Mama? What happened?"

"Those men of y'alls bought me and Daddy a new house in Green Point, Brooklyn!"

I got them a nice ass single family home right there in Green Point. I knew they didn't want to leave Brooklyn. They had a roof terrace that had a view of Manhattan. They still lived in Bed-Stuy, and since Moet was everywhere with me, I didn't want to leave them in harm's way.

"What? You got them a house?" Moet and Monett asked at the same time, while looking at me and Hakeem.

We both shrugged our shoulders and smirked. They ran into each of our arms and smiled. Tammy had a huge smile on her face, as she watched us loving our women.

"Let's eat, because I am too happy right now," Tammy said, and got up.

Christmas was a big ass success and I was happy. We ate, laughed and chilled until everyone left. It was just me and my baby in our home, which felt like everything.

"Baby, I appreciate everything you do," she rubbed my chest and kissed me, while she laid on my chest. I flipped her on top of me and started to take her shirt off, but she stopped.

"Come on, Moe… I want some of you. Since you've been pregnant, you haven't been wanting to let me hit that," I complained, and looked at her.

"I told you what it is, Zyair. If you're mad, then I don't know what to tell you!" she yelled, and rolled off of me.

I heard the door slam, and I knew I wasn't getting any. I turned the TV up and laid down, while watching a movie. I wasn't about to stress that right now. I closed my eyes and soon fell asleep.

*

Moet's stubborn ass didn't even come out the room, so I went to head to the gym with Hakeem. He swore since and he and Monett moved in together, she was losing weight and he was gaining it, because she cooked every day. I left some money and a note and headed out. Her and this attitude had me feeling some way. We were about to be married in a month and some weeks, and she was acting like this. Navi was headed in the building as I was leaving. I appreciated her for doing this wedding stuff. I paid her well because she was the best at what she did. How could I complain? I couldn't, because Navi was that good.

"Heading to the gym?" she asked, stepping through the door I held open for her.

"Yeah, you know… gotta keep it right. What y'all up to today?"

She looked through her calendar and sighed. "We're doing floral arrangements and invitations."

"Cool, cool."

"Oh, wait… Remember when you gave me the alright to start doing television appearances?"

"You mean what you forced me to do," I chuckled, and she laughed.

"Yeah that… Well, *The Voice* just called and wants you to fill Gwen Stefani's chair for three weeks. You know she's going through things with her soon-to-be husband."

"Damn, Moe ain't gonna be with that."

"I know, we have a lot of planning to do, so she can only come and visit, but coming with you isn't a choice. Plus, she's getting so involved with Monett's modeling too."

"Shit, try and mention it and I'll talk about it when I get home."

"I'm glad you don't want to cancel. The way I pulled strings for this boy," she laughed and headed upstairs.

I hopped in the awaiting car and was taken to the gym. Shit, I had to leave my baby to go film this. I wanted to step into entertainment a little bit. Hakeem actually suggested it and then Navi damn near threatened me to do it. Boxing wasn't forever and I eventually had to retire, so I always wanted to have a back-up plan, especially since I had a wife and baby on the way. A nigga had to think smart.

When I arrived at the gym, I started working out without Hakeem. His ass came strolling in an hour late with McDonalds.

"My bad, I overslept. Monett been really thanking a nigga since yesterday," he laughed.

"Yeah, when that big ass gut start to appear you gonna think twice 'bout that fast food," I shot back, and started running on the treadmill.

"So, did Navi speak to you about that?" He referred to what Navi had just spoken to me about.

"Yeah, got poor Navi doing your dirty work."

"I knew you wouldn't take it coming from me. You know her little ass is scary. But, I'm glad you're doing it."

"I know, the only positive thing about it is I could spend some time with Big Mama."

"See, it will all worked out. A nigga tired as hell, Monett is a freak."

"Tell her ass to hand her sister her freak powers back. Moet ain't gave me no ass since she found out she's pregnant."

"Damn, even after her gift? Shit, maybe she really scared about being pregnant."

"Yeah, I know. I need to stop being like that with her. That's my baby and she's carrying my baby, so I gotta check that ego at the door."

"My nigga, see, now go home and make that shit right."

"Yeah, later… grab something so we can get this real workout in," I laughed and he groaned.

I planned to break the news to my baby and make her feel better. We were six days to the new year and I wanted to bring it in right.

Chapter Eight

Monett

"Three, two, one…Happy New Years!" We all screamed and kissed each other. I kissed Hakeem and Nauti. Moet kissed Zane, and Tammy kissed Rick and Dion.

"It's been a hell of a year. I met my baby and we're about to have a baby, then walk down the aisle. I love you, Moet," I said and we shared a kiss.

"Y'all moved too damn fast, but I love my girl and I wouldn't have picked a better person for you, big head."

"Love you, lemon head."

"Now, I wanna say I am happy to be standing next to my baby because we thought that wouldn't be possible. I love you so much, Rich, and I am happy we're about to welcome another baby into our little family," she kissed him.

"I appreciate y'all for the support and shit… but this ain't 'bout me," Rick blushed, and we laughed. He was the sweetest and humblest man I knew.

After we put the kids to sleep, we sat on their balcony and looked at the confetti come down, since Zane and Moet's penthouse was right on Times Square. I sat on Hakeem's lap, and we drank champagne straight from the bottle. Moet and Tammy were standing by the rails talking and laughing, while Rick and Zane were shooting dice and throwing money down. You could take the man out the hood, but not the hood out the man. Hakeem kissed me before he went over to get on the game.

"What you heifers doing?" I asked, and looked at them smiling.

"The wedding and stuff. I just wanna be married and then deliver my baby already."

"Don't rush, Moe. Enjoy the experience," I said and hugged her.

"Yeah, I feel you. So, I hear Matt got you to model for top shop… That's big," she squealed and I blushed.

Since I handed Matt that contract, he took off running and started booking me so much stuff. The fact that Hakeem started acting like my manager didn't bother me either. He booked me for so much stuff for 2016, my head was spinning. We agreed to get a nanny, so that Nauti could come wherever I went. I also planned to let him stay with my mother sometimes too. Since Johnathan texted me that day, I hadn't heard from him. He claimed he wanted to be a parent.

"Yeah, he's been working super hard."

"I'm proud of your little skinny self," Tammy hugged her.

"Thanks boo!"

"Everything good with Rick?" Moet asked, and Tammy sighed.

"He has to do the surgery, but she says he'll be good and continue heeling after. I'm just so happy he's progressing. The nigga's bent down shooting dice, let that had been a couple months ago."

We laughed because only Tammy could make us laugh like that. "That's my brother and I need to make sure he's straight."

"You know it, baby cakes," they slapped hands and laughed.

We all hung out until around five in the morning. We headed home, and got Nauti back to sleep before we got to fucking. I swear I loved my man and his member. I could ride that shit all day if I could. Plus, I kept my calorie watch on when we fucked and a bitch was burning calories when I rode that magic stick. He picked me up and carried me to the room. I closed the door and got on the bed. I was ready to feel my man inside of me.

*

I slowed down from jogging so I could get inside our building. I checked the mail, while jogging in place and headed to our apartment. Nauti was with my mother, so I had some free time before I picked him up. We were two days into the new year and everything felt so right. I had a healthy baby, a good man and a two homes. God was definitely in the business of blessing my life. I threw the mail down and went to take off these sweaty clothes so I could shower. I was obsessed with keeping this body right, and making sure I looked good for my shoots.

After I finished in the shower, I went to get lunch together for Hakeem. He left out early this morning, so I knew he didn't pick nothing up to eat. I grabbed the mail and sorted his things and mine. I came across a golden envelope. I opened it and my eyes scanned across the paper. I dropped the paper and my chest started tightening. I dialed Moet's number so quick my fingers almost fell off.

"Aye, what's up?" she answered, chewing in my ear.

"Johnathan is taking me for joint custody of, Nauti!" I yelled.

Moet

"What do you mean for a couple weeks? Am I supposed to plan this wedding alone, Zyair?" I yelled, and he ignored me.

I walked in front of him and looked in his face. He was trying hard not to yell at me, but I could tell he wanted to. "Moet, I got to go and do this. You think I want to? I don't, but I gotta make this bread."

"So where does that leave me, us?"

"The same place, we're good. You can come back and forth and so can I."

I sighed in frustration and walked away. "I don't have time for this today!" I yelled.

He pulled me in his arms and kissed my neck. "I can make you better, baby," he moaned in my ear, and I shoved him off me and got up.

"Everything isn't about sex, Zyair!"

"Shit, I don't know how it could be when you never give me any. Damn, I wanna feel and touch my fiancée and she don't want me to. I'll call you when we take off," he said and grabbed his wallet, then walked towards the door. He stopped and came back and then kissed me on the lips before leaving.

Everything was happening so fast and didn't prepare us. Johnathan was taking Monett to court, Tammy had Rick going into surgery next week, and now Zyair wanted to take a gig that would take him away from home. I laid back on the bed, frustrated with all of this. I was cramping and went to the doctor earlier, and he said everything was good. I didn't want to have sex and then something happened. I knew he was getting frustrated with me. We were too new to be going through the no sex thing, but in order for me to bring this child into the world, that's what I had to do. I closed my eyes and went to sleep.

I don't know what time it was, but my phone was ringing and the house phone was ringing. I grabbed the phone and saw it was night time. I had slept until three in the morning.

"Hello?"

"Damn, I've been calling you for hours. You good, bae?"

"Yeah, I fell asleep… You there?"

"Yeah, and Big Mama making us dinner. Me and her need to talk."

"Yeah, y'all do. Tell her I said hey, and I'm going back to sleep."

"Love you."

"Love you too." We ended the call and I cuddled under the cover and went back to sleep. I had a lot of wedding things to do in the morning.

*

"I'm glad you decided to come with me. These things take forever," Tammy said, as we sat in the doctor's office. Rick was getting pre-op tests done before his surgery.

We were sitting and talking about anything, so we could entertain ourselves. "Me too, you know Zyair is in Cali, right?"

"When did he leave?"

"Yesterday. He's going to be on *The Voice*," I revealed and she clapped.

"Now that's my show, so he better do it justice," she snapped her neck.

"Tamala!"

She laughed. "You know I'm playing. You go visit your man, and make his ass come home. He doesn't wanna come to cake tasting; take the cake to him and let him taste it off those nipples."

I laughed, but that would only lead to sex. "I hear you."

"Boo, y'all will be fine, so knock it off."

"Thanks, boo. Sometimes I just don't know." We hugged and continued chatting, while waiting for Rick.

Tammy

I held Rick's hand, as they prepped him for surgery. This was his second surgery. His first one went good, but there was another bone that needed to be tended to. I wasn't worried, since his first one went well. However, his mother had said her dramatic well wishes and kissed him. The bitch took twenty minutes and everything. I kissed his lips a few times before handing Dion to him for him to kiss her.

"I love y'all for real, you hear me?" he said, and I kissed his lips again.

"Baby, we love you too. We need you to go ahead and do this so we can take you home."

"For real! You gonna cook?"

I laughed and kissed him. I couldn't get enough kisses. "Whatever ya greedy ass wants, I will give you."

"That's my baby." He grabbed my ass, and the nurses laughed.

"Okay, we'll take him to finish getting prepped. We'll update you every few hours, but it shouldn't take that long."

"Sounds good."

"Love you, baby…" I said, and hugged him.

"Ma, you know I love the shit out of you. You're my ride or die, Tam. I love all of my babies!" He kissed my stomach, me and then Dion.

"We love you baby." They rolled him to the back and Dion waved at her daddy. Rick's mother was taking her, so I could wait with Moet.

*

I sat in the family waiting room laying in Moet's lap. Rick had gone into surgery six hours ago, and I still hadn't been updated on anything. I was worried out my mind and couldn't sit still. Moet had finally convinced me to lay on her lap and take a quick nap, so I would be refreshed to bother Rick when he woke up. I laid on her lap, rubbing my stomach. People didn't lie when they said each pregnancy was different. I was fat, hungry and this little girl was weighing on my bladder. I couldn't wait to deliver and see my baby girl's face. I hoped like hell she looked more like me, because I couldn't take another light-skinned muthafucka in my house. I felt Moet rubbing my hair and humming. Since her miscarriage, she and Zyair barely spoke and he was mostly in California. They called the wedding off, and didn't hardly speak, unless it had to do with the bills. She had a beautiful seven-hundred-thousand-dollar dress sitting in the middle of their living room. She started back busting her ass at work, I guess to keep herself busy.

I told her she was engaged and needed to stop blaming that man. I could tell what I said went in one ear and right out the other. She wasn't trying to hear anything I was saying, especially with me being pregnant. I spoke to Zyair occasionally, and he was chilling. He said he wasn't about to be blamed for something he didn't do maliciously. Apparently, when Moet went to go visit Zyair, they missed each other so much that it led to sex. She claims he talked her into it. When she woke up the next morning, there was blood all over the bed, so she blames him for losing their child. Meanwhile, Moet was about a couple weeks along, and it could have been anything. But I guess she took comfort in blaming someone, and that someone was her fiancé.

They both were hardheaded and needed to put their situation to the side and be there for each other. Monett was still dealing with the situation with Johnathan. Everyone told her she needed to play dirty just like he was. She needed to speak the real truth about how he beat her. Yet, she claimed she wasn't going to stoop to his level. Because of that, there was a chance she would have to allow him to have joint custody of her child, but that's another story and that's for her to tell you.

I heard the door open and looked up. Dr. Hanna and another doctor walked over to us, and I sat up. She sat down across from us, and touched my hand.

"I'm sorry, Mrs. Smith," she started, and my voice was stuck in my throat. It was like a box juice, and you're trying to stab your straw through, but it won't go through. It was stuck, and I couldn't speak. My heart was beating a mile a minute, as I listened to her speak and explain how she killed my husband. "Everything was going as planned, but Rick had what we call a bleeder. The tumors were so overgrown and large, that we cut a blood vessel in the process. We tried to control it, however, it was uncontrollable. We're so sorry for your loss. If you would like to see him, we'll take you to him," she sincerely said, and patted my shoulder.

The straw broke through the juice box, and my voice came out squealing. I hadn't even noticed Moet crying hysterically, because I wailed like a dying dog. I fell from the chair onto the floor and screamed to the high heavens. This had to be a dream. My roll dog, husband, lover and ride or die since high school, couldn't be gone. We had two daughters to raise, send to college and be there for. How could he just give up and just leave me?

"H…How?!" I screamed, as I felt Moet put her arms around me. This was my sister right here. She could be anywhere, but she was on this floor with me with tears streaming down her face.

"Baby, you're going to be alright… I promise," she sniffled, as the tears fell onto the back of my neck.

"Moe, he's gone! My baby is fuckin' gone! Nothing is going to be alright, nothing!" I screamed into my lap.

I couldn't breathe. I literally felt like the air had been kicked out of my body. How was I supposed to go home to my daughter who looked just like him? Walk in a house that had our smell? Every place in our house reminded me of him. It was our house; he was the king of our castle.

"Please Tam, please," she begged while trying to console me, but I was sprawled out on the floor, bawling like a big ass baby. I just kept replaying our last moments together and it brought so many tears to my eyes.

"I…I need to see him," I cried, and she helped me off the floor. My swollen belly leading the way, was another reminder of my husband.

We walked slowly down the hall and came to a closed door. "Take all the time you need," Dr. Hanna softly said, and opened the door.

I turned the corner and broke down. Rick was lying there in the hospital bed as if he was sleeping. He was still hooked up to machines, and his chest was pumping up and down. Tubes were coming out his mouth. He looked as if he was taking a nap, not dead. I slowly walked into the room, and looked toward the door. Moet was standing there with tears in her eyes and Dr. Hanna looked like she was close to tears. I walked to him and touched his arms. He was still warm like the blood was still shooting through his body.

"B…baby," I chocked out, as I moved his blanket and climbed into bed with him. His body was stiff as a board, but I climbed into that bed and cuddled like we did so many times.

"She cant d-" The other doctor, an intern I assumed was about to say.

"She just lost her husband, she can do whatever the hell she wants to do. You know what? Go find me all his files, so I can go over what went wrong," I heard the doctor tell the intern. I laid my head on his chest and felt so at peace. In my mind, he was just taking a quick rest and he would be up soon.

"We've checked and he's a donor… He has twenty-four hours before we have to retrieve the organs, so she can take her time with him… Again, I am so sorry."

"Thank you," Moet sniffled, and I sobbed into his chest. I couldn't stop crying, and feeling him and smelling him, but not being able to take him home was driving me insane. Who would have thought we would shower, lay in our bed and eat breakfast for the last time together? I laid there and got as comfortable as my belly would allow me. I wasn't moving from my baby, at all!

Moet

Tammy wanted to be left alone with Rick's body. I cried, begged and pleaded with her to come get some fresh air, and she refused. The doctors were due to take him in a little while, and she didn't want to leave. She had been in that room for over sixteen hours without getting up to eat, shower or pee. Her face was red and her eyes were swollen shut. I hadn't left her side since we found out, and I didn't plan to. She told me not to call anyone, and if I did, then I was dead to her. I knew she was speaking on emotion, but I had to respect her wishes. At the same time, I couldn't help but feel for his mother. She had been calling Tammy's phone repeatedly. This was too much for me and I felt like I was breaking down. Rick was like a big brother to me. Anything I needed, he was there. When Tammy and I went through our little fights, he was the listening ear for both of us. My heart ached that my best friend lost a piece of her.

I didn't know where Zyair and I stood anymore. When we talked, it was about the things that had to be handled. I barely stayed at the penthouse. I was back at my parents' house and working all the time. Whenever I did call him, it went to voicemail and then I would see him hosting a party. He told me he didn't even like doing those things and would never do them, but I see people change. Big Mama called me and checked up one me from time to time. I still wore my engagement ring, because I assumed we were together. Now, I didn't know anymore. He never broke it off officially, but he didn't talk about me in the media either. People were questioning if we were even together anymore. I know I was dumb for blaming him about the miscarriage, because the doctor had told me ahead of time that it might happen. He said my HCG levels were low, which meant I would soon be having a miscarriage. I'm one of those people that when things don't make sense, I have to blame someone so that it could all come full circle for me. Zyair happened to be that person, so I blamed him. I blamed him so bad, that I was crying and feeling bad about it now.

Why did it have to take a tragedy for people to open their eyes? Now in hindsight, I could see what I did was stupid and I should have been there with my man, instead of checking out the hospital, while he went home to get me clothes, and getting a flight back home without him knowing. He lost a baby too; it wasn't just about me, and that's what I made it about. I walked outside and plopped down on the bench with tears on my cheeks. My life was in a shambles right now. When I was at work, I wasn't mentally there. My relationship was on the rocks, and my best friend was going through one of the most horrible things in her life. I rumbled through my pocket and pulled out my cell phone. I dialed Zyair's number and waited for him to answer. The tears slid down my cheeks at the thought of what went on in the last sixteen hours. I just wanted to be in his arms.

"Quit playing, Zane…Hello?" a woman giggled into the phone; I dropped the phone.

To Be Continued ….

Will the lawsuit money come in after Rick's death? Will Monett finally reveal to her family about Johnathan almost killing her and Nauti? Will she play dirty and pull out the proof of all of Johnathan's abuse? Is Zane cheating on Moet? Will Tammy heal? Or will Rick's family come for his settlement, if she gets it? Will Zane and Moet make it down the aisle? Will this break them?

Text ROYALTY to 42828 to keep up with our new releases!

ROYALTY
PUBLISHING HOUSE

Be sure to LIKE our Royalty Publishing House page on Facebook

CPSIA information can be obtained
at www.ICGtesting.com
Printed in the USA
LVHW05s1636241018
594669LV00009B/656/P

9 781522 813835